"You weren't my doctor, but I noticed you."

Brady smiled; there was that dimple again. "I secretly hoped that you noticed me, too. But I get it. There are so many patients, we become a number."

"You certainly weren't a number." Sheila took the wounded bull rider's hand. She braved a look into his eyes.

Suddenly she rose, pulling away from him. "What am I doing?"

"I'm sorry. I shouldn't have told you that."

Sheila shook her head. "You understand that nothing can ever happen between us? It would cost me my job. Nobody is worth that sacrifice."

"Relax, Doc." Brady shrugged. "It was just a harmless flirtation. It won't happen again."

"Good." His admission was oddly reassuring and uncomfortable at the same time. "I'm going to finish my rounds and then I'll be back to see you."

Brady winked. "I'll be here when you're ready."

Sheila shouldn't have read anything into his reply, but the under~~current was undeniable~~ ~~an had~~ ever h~~~~ ~~~~'t carefu

A BULL RIDER'S PRIDE

BY
AMANDA RENEE

MILLS
BOON

First Published in Great Britain 2016
By Mills & Boon, an imprint of HarperCollins*Publishers*
1 London Bridge Street, London, SE1 9GF

© 2016 Amanda Renee

ISBN: 978-0-263-92013-0

23-0816

Our policy is to use papers that are natural, renewable and recyclable products and made from wood grown in sustainable forests. The logging and manufacturing processes conform to the legal environmental regulations of the country of origin.

Printed and bound in Spain
by CPI, Barcelona

Amanda Renee was raised in the Northeast and now wriggles her toes in the warm sand of coastal South Carolina. Her career began when she was discovered through Mills & Boon's So You Think You Can Write contest. When not creating stories about love and laughter, she enjoys the company of her schnoodle, Duffy, camping, playing guitar and piano, photography and anything involving horses. You can visit her at www.amandarenee.com.

For Dad
Thank you for always supporting me.
I love you.

Prologue

The roar of the crowd faded as he sailed through the air. Gravity defying seconds morphed into an eternity until he struck the dirt with a resounding thud. A frenzy of blurred images danced before him in the deafening silence. He scrambled to his knees, searching for the safety of the arena fence. Muted shouts began to seep through the murkiness. Adrenaline triumphed over the growing ache that tore through his left leg. Then darkness overshadowed him. Once more, he was plucked effortlessly from the ground like a twig in a summer twister. The bull's head slammed into his spine—the sudden blow burning his lungs.

His arms desperately clawed for something to hold on to as the bull violently swung his head from side to side, but he found only the beast beneath him. With each twist and snort, the animal stole another breath from his body. And then nothing.

No sound.

No pain.

His world slipped away with a single thought... *Gunner.*

Chapter One

"I'll never understand what motivates someone to climb on top of a one-ton animal hell-bent to drive them into the ground." Orthopedic surgeon Dr. Sheila Lindstrom reviewed Brady Sawyer's chart one final time before she headed down the hall to give him the news he'd been waiting two months to hear.

"Bull riders are nothing more than stubborn cowboys looking for an adrenaline fix," Marissa Sloane said. The junior orthopedic surgical resident assigned to Sheila's service at Grace General Hospital tossed her coffee cup in the trash behind the nurse's station and scanned the patient whiteboard. "Look at it this way, bull riding helps keep us in business. Besides, I think you have a soft spot for the cowboy. You've monitored his case ever since he was admitted and he wasn't even your patient. Well, at least not until today."

"Only because I was on rotation that night and assisted on his initial surgery." The trauma team had airlifted Brady from the arena and he'd coded once while en route. "I'm still amazed he made it through the first twenty-four hours, let alone is strong enough for release to a rehabilitation facility." Sheila was glad she'd been wrong. Seeing a patient leave the hospital in remarkably better condition than when they arrived was its own reward.

"And you get to go with him." Marissa playfully elbowed her.

"I'm hardly going with him. The hippotherapy center is part of my job." The orthopedic surgeon residency program provided services free of charge to the Dance of Hope Hippotherapy Center located fifteen minutes away in Ramblewood, Texas. The facility, which used horses' movements to treat a number of conditions, had been a huge incentive when Sheila interviewed for the residency program four years earlier. "Double-check the OR schedule for me and see if there've been any changes. I'm scheduled for an arthroscopic rotator cuff repair this morning."

"It doesn't hurt that he's extremely good-looking." Marissa logged into the hospital's electronic medical records system. "You're still set for nine o'clock."

Sheila checked her watch. It was six in the morning and she'd already put in two hours. "I didn't notice his looks." That wasn't entirely true. She'd noticed Brady's handsome features almost immediately. His face was one of the few body parts he hadn't injured. The same couldn't be said for his head. After registering only a seven out of fifteen on the Glasgow Coma Scale due to an epidural hematoma, his survival outlook had been grim. It had taken a dozen surgeries to save his life and get him to the point where he could be released to Dance of Hope.

"Lindstrom, I need an assist on an ACL reconstruction." Dr. Mangone, their attending physician, approached. "It's your call."

"I'm certain Dr. Sloane here is up for it. I have a rotator cuff this morning." Sheila noticed Marissa's subtle happy dance out of the corner of her eye. Trying not to smile, she focused her attention on Dr. Mangone. "I'm discharging Brady Sawyer this morning."

"Ah, our resident cowboy. I'll be glad to see him go. In my thirty-six years of practice, I don't think I've ever seen a more—how should I put this—*determined* patient. I just hope he doesn't overdo it at Dance of Hope. I'm not a hundred percent comfortable with his therapy taking place on the back of a horse. Especially when he's so fixated on competing again."

"I've already discussed his condition with the staff," Sheila said. "But I'll be sure to reiterate his limitations... and his determination, as you so graciously put it. Not that I think it will stop him." Brady Sawyer had developed a bit of a reputation around Grace General during his stay. The nurses commonly referred to him as Superman. From the day he awoke from his two-week coma, he'd vowed to get back in the ring and unfailingly pushed himself. Marissa was right—he was one stubborn cowboy.

"You see to it that he doesn't come back here. I've operated on him enough," Dr. Mangone said. "Sloane, scrub in."

Sheila proceeded down the hallway toward Brady's room. It was early, but most patients were already awake since the nurses had begun their rounds. Although she was dying for a caffeine fix, she decided to hold off until after she told him the good news. She hated talking to patients with coffee still lingering on her breath. She hesitated at his door, smoothing the front of her scrubs and inwardly laughed. Despite what Marissa had implied, she did not have a soft spot for the cowboy.

While Brady Sawyer was no stranger to her, she doubted he remembered any of their previous meetings during his two-and-a-half-month hospital stay. Dr. Mangone had been his physician until yesterday when he'd handed her the reins. Sheila pushed open the door to Brady's room and was surprised to see it empty.

She stopped a nurse in the hallway. "Where's Mr. Sawyer?"

"Probably in the atrium. He likes to go there and watch the sunrise every morning. Would you like me to get him?"

"No, I don't mind the walk." Grace General's atrium was a favorite with visitors and staff. Located in the center of the hospital, it had five-story glass walls facing east and west along with a glass panel ceiling. Lush green trees grew around the center fountain giving it a parklike appearance. The morning light created an ethereal haze over the area and there Brady sat in his wheelchair staring out the window, a slight smile on his cleanly shaven face. The sun peeked over the horizon, casting golden shadows across the parking lot. Dressed in black sweatpants and a black T-shirt, he looked as if he was ready to go for a morning jog despite being restricted to a wheelchair.

"Do you ever take a moment and just watch the sunrise?" He asked without even looking at her. "I never took the time to really notice it until I came here."

"Normally, I'm on rounds at this time." Sheila sat down in the chair next to him. "Enjoy the sunrise, Mr. Sawyer because it will be the last one you ever see here."

Immediately Sheila noticed Brady's jaw tense. "This is the one moment of enjoyment I have out of my entire day and you're going to take that away from me?" Brady faced her. His blue-gray eyes met hers with intensity.

"In a sense, yes I am." Sheila smiled and held out her hand. "I'm Dr. Lindstrom and I'm releasing you today."

Brady grasped her hand between both of his. His face lit, exposing tiny creases near his temples. "You really mean it? The other day Dr. Mangone said he wasn't sure how much longer I'd be here."

Sheila knew she shouldn't revel in the feel of his touch, but the fact that he still hadn't let go of her hand made it next to impossible. The strength and vitality he had compared to the night he was brought in bordered on miraculous. This was the first time she'd seen Brady up close outside of the operating room. The morning sun on his short dark hair brought out hints of gold she hadn't noticed from afar. Marissa was right again. He was extremely good-looking.

"Mr. Sawyer—"

"Please, call me Brady."

"Okay, Brady." Sheila eased her hand from his grip. "Dr. Mangone transferred your case to me and I'll be monitoring your progress at the Dance of Hope Hippotherapy Center. I understand you're aware of the program and all it entails. It's still in-house physical therapy—much like the program you're in here—only utilizing horses. It's my understanding a social worker has spoken with you about residing in one of their on-site cottages during rehabilitation. They have an opening and are expecting you today. Can I tell them you'll take it?"

"Absolutely! I live alone and my father's farmhouse is two stories. Neither place is exactly wheelchair accessible." Brady rolled his chair backward and forward anxiously. "Not that I'll be in this thing much longer."

Sheila clenched her teeth and forced a smile. "Mr. Sawyer—Brady—while Dance of Hope is an amazing facility, we can't predict what result the therapy will have. I admire your determination, and believe me when I say it goes a long way, but you need to be realistic with your goals."

Brady's face lost all amusement. "My goal is to compete again as soon as possible. One accident won't stop me."

Sheila rolled her shoulders. She'd heard the nurses talk about Brady's desire to get back on a bull, but she'd thought the reality of his prognosis would've set in by now. "I respect and even understand your wanting to compete again, but another injury—"

Brady held up his hand, effectively cutting her off. "Please don't. I have already heard the 'if the bull's horn was an inch more to the left it would have pierced your heart' speech a hundred times. It didn't. I'm still here. And I'm going to make the best of each day, and that includes riding to win."

Sheila rose and stood behind his wheelchair. "Don't make me regret releasing you today." She began to push him out of the atrium, ignoring when he attempted to do it himself. "We'll contact Dance of Hope and arrange your transport. You'll be ready to go once I've given you a final exam and your discharge papers are complete." Sheila slammed into the back of his chair, almost launching herself over him.

"I can wheel myself, thank you." Brady released the brake and began wheeling ahead of her. "Didn't anyone ever tell you it's rude to push someone in a wheelchair without their approval?"

Sheila stood in the middle of the atrium, speechless. Determination was one thing, but Brady Sawyer brought a new definition to the word and it wasn't pretty.

BRADY DESPISED FEELING HELPLESS. Between his father, Alice—who was his best friend and his son's mother—and his friends, somebody was always trying to do something for him. He needed to do things for himself—he wanted to. And that included maneuvering his own wheelchair. If Dr. Lindstrom hadn't been so attractive he probably would've realized what she was about to do and stopped her. But her soft silver eyes had captured his attention and held it until she'd started arguing with him about competing. He'd already heard it from everybody else. It would be nice if other people believed in him the way his four-year-old son did. Gunner was his biggest supporter and the only one who still had faith in him.

Brady barreled into his hospital room and spun his chair around to face the door before Dr. Lindstrom arrived. He squeezed his eyes shut willing himself to get through the next few hours. They were finally releasing him. He'd dreamed of hearing that phrase, yet he'd been completely unprepared for it. Especially when it came from the beautiful doctor he'd watched from afar throughout his stay.

"You're right." Dr. Lindstrom stood in the doorway. "That was very rude of me and I apologize. If you'll humor me, just for a second, maybe I can explain where I'm coming from. I promise it won't be a lecture."

Brady nodded. He propped his left elbow up on the arm of his chair, running the back of his fingers across his chin. Sure, he could listen for a few minutes in exchange for his freedom. Regardless of what she or anyone else said, failure wasn't an option. He realized the odds were against him, but this was the only job he knew.

Dr. Lindstrom entered the room with a nurse in tow. *Safety in numbers.* Maybe he had been a little too harsh in the atrium.

"As your physician, I want you to recover as completely as your body will allow. In order to do that we need to set a series of attainable goals so you're consistently seeing improvement. Of course I want you to strive for the best possible scenario, but when you set extremely high goals from the outset, it tends to hinder recovery. The human body has a remarkable way of rebuilding itself—"

"Then you understand the ability to recover and return to a normal life."

Sheila grimaced. "I understand the body's ability to heal, yes. And many patients do go on to live normal lives. Not all of them, though. Some must learn to adjust."

She sighed. "I've sacrificed a lot to become an orthopedic surgeon—my family, friends, social life, not to mention four hundred thousand dollars in student loans I still have to repay. I was one of the surgeons who put you back together—you were on the operating table for fifteen hours. I tend to get a little frustrated when a patient wants to put himself in the same environment that brought him here in the first place."

Well that made him feel like a first-class ass. "Don't get me wrong, Dr. Lindstrom. I respect your point of view. All I ask is that you respect mine, as well."

Dr. Lindstrom's lips thinned. She opened a large envelope the nurse handed her and crossed the room to the light box on the wall. Turning it on, she held up his films. "These are from your CT scans yesterday. Your hip replacement healed beautifully. You're lucky you're in a facility that uses the anterior approach because your recovery would've been much longer if it had been performed the traditional way. Your broken clavicle, sternum and left humerus look good. The fact you can wheel yourself all over this hospital proves your shoulder surgeries were a success. I understand from your physical therapist that you're still feeling tightness in your thighs, left knee and spinal regions."

"It's not so much tightness as it is weakness." Brady

attempted to sit taller in his chair. "I can stand, but I tire quickly."

Dr. Lindstrom slid the scans back into the envelope and handed it to the nurse. "Let's take a look." She walked to him, checked the brakes on his wheelchair and held out both of her hands for him to hold on to. "Don't worry, I'm stronger than I look, I won't let you fall."

I won't let you fall. Brady had said those same words to Gunner when he was learning to walk. Now here he was, a twenty-nine-year-old man learning to walk again.

"Brady, most of the therapists at Dance of Hope are women. If this is going to be a problem—"

"No." Brady met her eyes and reached for her. "It's not a problem. I just—I needed a second." Her touch was stronger, more deliberate than when she'd introduced herself earlier. He didn't doubt her strength or ability to support him. He doubted his resolve to not want more of it.

Her cheeks darkened to a deep crimson—perhaps she sensed his attraction to her. "Take your time," she reassured. "I've got you."

Brady stared at her hospital identification badge as he slowly stood. Her photograph made him momentarily forget the shaking in his legs. She looked different with her dark hair down around her shoulders. Every time he'd seen her, it had always been either in a ponytail or a braid of some sort. Sheila. Her name was Sheila. He'd never known a Sheila before. It suited her.

She cleared her throat. His gaze immediately flew to hers and then back to her badge, which he realized rested right against her left breast. "I wasn't looking at your— Your badge… I was looking at your badge."

Sheila started to laugh. "It's all right, Brady." She took a step closer, offering him more support. "How does that feel?"

That was a loaded question. It felt amazing standing less than a foot away from her. Feeling her hands in his. She was tall. Taller than he'd thought from the vantage point of his chair. Maybe only four or five inches shorter than his six-foot-two frame. And she didn't smell as he'd imagined. Whenever he'd seen her, he'd thought of honeysuckle for some reason. Her scent was more of freshly laundered cotton sheets.

"Brady?"

That feeling he had forgotten a few seconds ago suddenly came back. "Not as steady as I'd like, but better than yesterday."

"Do you feel any pain?"

Brady shook his head. "I think I stopped noticing pain a month ago."

"Okay, you can take a seat." Sheila waited until he was in his chair before releasing his hands. "Hippotherapy will greatly strengthen your core and leg muscles. I'm going to discharge you today with the understanding that you adhere to the program at Dance of Hope. I will be closely monitoring your progress and I'll be checking in with you when I make my rounds there. Don't overdo it, Brady. I don't want to admit you back into this hospital again."

"I'll be good, Doc." Brady winked, then instantly regretted it when the nurse giggled. There was nothing like a disabled man flirting with a gorgeous doctor. "You won't recognize me the next time you see me."

Sheila's brows rose. "I don't know if I should be scared by that statement or not. Just remember, I'll be watching you." She made a V with her fingers and waved them between her eyes and his. "Take care, Brady. I'll see you soon."

Brady was torn between wanting to see her right away and wanting to wait until he could do more than stand on wobbly legs. He knew she doubted he'd make a full recovery, but he'd prove her wrong. And then, maybe he'd even ask her out.

Chapter Two

Sheila stripped out of her operating-room scrubs and tossed them into the hospital laundry bin. By the time she'd finished with her rotator-cuff reconstruction, Brady had been discharged and was on his way to Dance of Hope. Anyone who had one of the world's most dangerous jobs definitely had the dedication it took to recover from his injuries. But a full recovery was doubtful. And she didn't want Brady to become disillusioned if his body didn't bounce back the way he hoped.

The thought of Brady being disappointed or giving up because he could not ride a bull bothered her more than it should. She'd learned during her first year internship to compartmentalize her emotions. Regardless of how hard she tried, she couldn't save all of them and there were lots of Brady Sawyers in the world. Men determined to push their bodies further than they were meant to go.

Sheila had made a note on his file to discuss readjustment counseling in the upcoming weeks. She preferred to allow a patient to progress further along in their therapy before making the recommendation. Her colleagues didn't always agree, but she felt mentioning it too soon shattered morale and hindered their improvement.

"Thanks for letting me take that surgery." Marissa entered the locker room. "We had a patellar fracture during the tendon harvest."

"You tend to see a lot of that in sports medicine," Sheila said. "I'm heading to the cafeteria. Care to join me?"

"Sure. How did it go with your cowboy?"

The question created a slight tingle in her belly. "He's not my cowboy." The image of him standing in front of her replayed in her brain. She shook her head in a vain attempt to rid herself of the memory. "After talking with him, I understand Dr. Mangone's trepidation about sending him to Dance of Hope. Brady's a bit too gung ho to climb back on a bull and the fact that the hippotherapy center is located next to a rodeo school concerns me."

"Brady?" Marissa stopped in the doorway and faced her. "It didn't take long to progress to first names."

Sheila pushed past her. "Don't even joke about that. He's a patient, Marissa. You know any romantic relationship is strictly forbidden by the medical board and this hospital. I'm not willing to risk my residency on anyone."

"Relax, I'm only teasing." Marissa held up her hands. "But if he wasn't your patient you'd be tempted, right?"

Sheila spun to face her. "Listen to me. I've come too far and worked too hard to jeopardize my career over a rumor. If the wrong person hears what you're saying, you could ruin everything for me. I'm trying to get into the orthopedic trauma fellowship program next year and I don't need this."

"Whoa. For someone with no romantic attachments to a patient you're certainly doing your damnedest to defend yourself."

She had every reason to. She'd almost given up medical school when her boyfriend asked her to move to Arizona. Fate had intervened and she'd caught him in bed with someone else, saving her from walking away from her dreams. Now she realized no amount of love or promise of a happily-ever-after was worth it. Relationships didn't last forever. Being a doctor would.

Before Sheila had the chance to argue her point further, both of their pagers went off. *Trauma Alert ER*. "Let's move!"

THE DANCE OF HOPE transport van pulled in front of the combined hippotherapy center and rodeo school entrance. The July sun warmed Brady's face as he eased his legs out of the van and stepped onto the ground using the door as support. A woman with close-cropped salt-and-pepper hair greeted him with a wheelchair.

"I'm Kay Langtry." She helped him into the chair. "It's a pleasure to meet you, Brady."

"Ma'am, it's a pleasure to be here."

"We promise to take good care of you during your stay. Since it's lunchtime, why don't I start our tour in the common dining area."

Brady hadn't realized how hungry he was. "Sounds good to me. Lead the way."

Kay nodded, silently acknowledging that he didn't need any assistance. He was sweating by the time they reached the center's entrance. It was the first time he'd used a wheelchair outside. The experience left him craving a cold shower rather than lunch. Brady paused in the entryway. He could hear the whoops and shouts coming from the rodeo school through massive oak doors to the right. He knew those sounds well and he missed them more than anything. The rodeo was his life—his past and his future.

"Do you need a moment?" Kay crouched down beside him so they were at eye level with one another. A gesture he appreciated. He got tired of always looking up at everyone, especially when he was used to towering over most people.

"I'm good. I'm anxious to get started." When Dr. Mangone had told him about the hippotherapy center, he'd hopped online to research it. He'd been relieved to discover it was less than an hour away from his father, son and Alice. "Visitors are allowed, right?"

"Yes, they are." Kay stood. "As often as you'd like. Let's grab a bite to eat and settle you in. Feel free to invite your family to join us for dinner tonight. We always have enough food around here."

"Thank you, I think I will."

The common dining area took Brady off guard. He'd seen photos of it online, but it had been empty then. He hadn't been prepared for the number of children in wheelchairs or on crutches. There were some military personnel—both men and women. That he'd expected. But the children broke his heart. Children Gunner's age.

"I know this can be unsettling at first." Kay placed a hand on his shoulder. "But don't ever tell anyone here that you feel sorry for them or show them any pity. You will find this to be a very grateful and determined group. Everyone has the same goal—to get out of here one day. Some will walk out, others won't. But it's a team effort and everybody is rooting for you."

Brady felt his heart pound in his chest. He was used to people rooting for him...in a different arena. He'd root for every child, every person here. As much as he wanted to be in his own home, he knew this was the best place for him. He would walk and compete again.

SHEILA SLAMMED HER front door. She'd lost a patient on the operating table. It happened often in trauma surgeries. She should be used to it by now. But how did someone get used to having a person with a family and a future breathing beneath their fingertips one minute and then gone the next along with all their hopes, all their dreams?

Sheila ran into the bathroom and splashed cold water on her face. It never got easier—you just grew more desensitized to it. Today had been particularly difficult—a ten-year-old girl with her whole future ahead of her. Dead thanks to her sister who had been texting and driving. The sister had survived, but would live with the consequences for the rest of her life.

This was why Sheila was so infuriated with Brady Sawyer. Most of her patients learned something from their experience. The overweight person with two knee replacements learned they had to move and exercise more. The kid with a fractured tibia learned not to attempt a flip-over-willy-grind skateboard trick down the school handrail. What did Brady Sawyer learn? Nothing.

And yes, there was a chance he'd fully recover. A very slim one, but with the proper therapy, the chance was real. Sheila had been a longtime proponent of hippotherapy and its benefits. Growing up in Colorado, she'd lived near a facility much like Dance of Hope. Few people had known much about hippotherapy and its benefits back then. When she turned fourteen, her parents had allowed her to volunteer there. There was an orthopedic surgeon who visited the facility every week and for four years she'd watched him restore quality of life back to people who'd felt as if their world had ended. He'd inspired her to go into medicine, particularly orthopedic trauma. Now she helped save lives like Brady's and he was all too willing to throw it away.

His attitude shouldn't bother her, but it did. And it would continue to bother her until he was no longer her patient, and then every time she saw a bull riding event on television she'd still wonder. Sheila laughed to herself. He wasn't her first bull rider and probably wouldn't be her last. She lived in the heart of Hill Country where rodeos were as common as apple pie. The suburban town she'd grown up in had been a stark contrast. She'd known many equestrians, but not bull riders.

Thinking of home reminded her it had been over a week since she'd last phoned her parents. Every night there was a message from them on her voice mail. Today she'd actually gotten off early enough to return the call.

"Hello, honey," her mom answered on the first ring. "How's our favorite surgeon?"

"It was a rough day. I lost a patient." No matter how difficult her residency was, she knew she could always turn to her mother for comfort.

"Oh honey, do you want to talk about it?" Sheila heard a muffled sound and assumed her mother had covered the receiver.

"Mom, tell Daddy later, and no, I don't want to talk about it. I'd rather hear about your day."

"Your sister had an ultrasound today—a three-dimensional one. You won't believe how much Sophia resembles you as a baby—that's the name they've chosen—did I tell you that already? Anyway, she posted the photos online. Look at them later if you get the chance. We'll be so glad when your residency is over next summer and you move home. You're missing your nieces and nephews growing up."

Sheila released her ponytail and flopped onto the couch. "About that. I've decided to pursue the two-year orthopedic trauma fellowship at Grace General."

"I thought you were looking into fellowships here." Disappointment was evident in her mother's tone.

"I know that was the plan, Mom, but this fellowship wasn't available until recently. I like Grace General and my work here. I'm looking to make this permanent. My landlord gave me the option to apply my rent toward a down payment on this house. It's not much but it's more than I can afford in Colorado. Once I weed through these student loans, then maybe, but I've given this a lot of thought and this is what's best for me."

"What about settling down and starting a family? You're not getting any younger."

Any comfort she'd hoped for had just flown out the window. "My social life consists of my colleagues. It's not as if I have much time or energy to go out and meet people. Besides children require much more than I'm able to give. Maybe in a few years I'll feel differently. I don't need a husband and kids to make me happy. I'm content with my life right now."

At least that was the lie she told herself every night before she went to bed. Sometimes she'd roll over in the middle of the night and reach out for someone who wasn't there. Her life severely lacked intimacy. The last hug she'd received had been from a patient after Sheila had given her good news. The last time someone other than a family member had said *I love you* had been her college boyfriend. And sex? She didn't want to think about how long that had been. Okay, so it bothered her, but she'd known this career path came with sacrifices. She'd accepted it. She just didn't exactly care for it.

"I want you to be happy, Sheila." Her mom's voice softened. "You need to call more often. We miss you."

"I miss you more."

After hearing about her father's new car, her mother's bridge-game gossip and more about her sister's third pregnancy, she poured herself a glass of wine and eased into a bubble bath. She closed her eyes and Brady Sawyer immediately came to mind.

"Dammit!" She sat up so quickly she knocked her

wine into the tub. "That's lovely." She'd touched him twice and she couldn't erase the feeling of his hands in hers. She turned her glass upright and set it on the floor. Grabbing a pumice stone, she ran it over her palms. Why was he haunting her? That was exactly how she felt. Haunted. Every time she closed her eyes, she saw him. And it wasn't just today. He'd been a daily thought for two and a half months. She constantly told herself she wasn't attracted to him. She couldn't be. It simply wasn't allowed and she chalked it up to curiosity about the man. But if Marissa had detected it so easily, she wondered who else had.

Brady Sawyer had left the building. With his drive and determination, he'd progress quickly at Dance of Hope and be out of her life for good. Which was for the best. So why did the thought of never seeing him again bother her?

"DON'T WORRY ABOUT the child-support payments. Focus on getting better." Alice sat on the bed across from Brady in his Dance of Hope cottage while Gunner played with his See & Spell at the table. "You're an amazing father and I know you want to do everything possible to make sure Gunner is provided for, and I promise you, if things get really bad I'll let you know. We're okay. It's tight, but we're managing. Your father checks in on us all the time."

"You shouldn't have to manage and my father shouldn't be the one providing for you." Brady gripped the arms of his wheelchair. He and Alice had never been a couple. They'd been best friends since childhood who happened to have spent one lonely night together that resulted in the most precious gift he could have ever received. Unfortunately, they hadn't any romantic feelings toward each other. So far, they'd successfully raised Gunner together, yet separately. "Why do you do this to me?"

"Why do I do what? Bring your son to see you? Because he loves you and he asks about you every day."

Brady wheeled closer to the bed so Gunner wouldn't hear him. "And a part of you secretly wishes that by seeing me in this condition he won't want anything to do with the rodeo."

"There might be some truth to that." Alice lowered her voice. "What mother doesn't want her child to be safe? You almost died, Brady. We keep telling you that, but it hasn't seemed to register in your brain yet. I don't want that future for our son. You already have him mutton busting and racing around the arena on miniature horses. I'm terrified of what comes next."

"The severity of my accident was highly unusual and you know it. I was a special circumstance." Brady had grown tired of defending himself to Alice and his father. At first he'd been disappointed when his father told him he couldn't make it tonight; now he was glad the two of them weren't together to gang up on him.

"You were only special because you survived. It was never a matter of if you'd get hurt, it was when you'd get hurt. I almost lost my best friend that day, but more important, Gunner almost lost his father. I get so angry when I hear you say you need to compete again in order to support him. You're using our son as an excuse. There are other ways to earn a living, so don't you dare tell me it's all for Gunner. I know better and so do you."

"You have no idea. Before they discharged me, I had to meet with the billing department. My insurance doesn't cover everything and if I don't pay, believe me they will come after me for their money. Every cent I have to pay them takes away from Gunner. Working minimum wage won't pay the bills, Alice. At least Dance of Hope didn't cost me anything." Brady had already promised to one day give back to the nonprofit dedicated to providing therapy to people regardless of their ability to pay.

"We both know this isn't just about money." Alice rested her hand on his. "You need to forgive yourself. Your mom wouldn't want you to carry around all this guilt."

He pulled away from her. His mother had died in her sleep while Brady and his father were away on a rodeo trip. He didn't want to think about that day, but the memory of finding her remained fresh in his mind every time he competed. Alice was right. It was about much more than the money. He rode for his mother. He rode for his father. And now, he rode for his son.

He wheeled over to the table. "Hey, champ, it's almost your bedtime. You and your mommy need to head home."

"I want to stay with you," Gunner pleaded.

Brady bit back the sob that threatened to break free. He wanted nothing more than to spend the night with his son. He missed their time together more than anything. "Daddy doesn't live here. I'm just visiting. Once I get home, you can stay with me anytime you want."

"Promise?" Gunner looked up at him with his big brown eyes.

He hated telling his son no. "I promise, little man. Things will be back to normal soon."

Brady had never broken a promise to his son, and he wouldn't start now.

THE FOLLOWING MORNING Brady awoke feeling more rested than he had in months—the ranch was dead silent at night in comparison to the constant bustle of the hospital. He'd almost been afraid to open his eyes out of fear his release had been a dream.

Over a hearty country breakfast, he reviewed the schedule Kay Langtry had given him the day before. Eager to begin his therapy, he hurriedly ate and wheeled to the main indoor hippotherapy arena.

A woman no more than an inch or two over five feet tall greeted him.

"Good morning, Brady. I'm Abby, your physical therapist."

"Are you sure you can support my weight?" Brady asked.

"Don't let my size fool you, and you're going to be supporting yourself the majority of the time. I know you're raring to get on a horse, but there are a few things we need to go over first." Abby marched to an oversize cabinet along the wall and opened it. "Rule number one—when you're in an arena, either indoors or out, a helmet must be worn at all times. No exceptions. No helmet, no hippotherapy."

Brady hated helmets. It had been a heavily debated issue throughout the industry for years and he'd always been against it. That didn't stop him from making Gunner wear one whenever he entered the ring. But considering he didn't want to end up back in the hospital, a helmet sounded like a good idea. "Agreed."

"Number two, it's my understanding your wheelchair usage has been limited to the smooth flat surfaces inside the hospital. Dance of Hope is situated on the Bridle Dance Ranch, which is a 250,000 acre paint and cutting horse ranch. You have access to many of the trails and I assure you, they're not smooth or flat."

"We're free to roam around?" Brady itched to do some exploring, especially with Gunner. They had always spent their father and son time together at rodeo events, fishing or trail riding. He'd missed that during his hospital stay.

Abby nodded. "Our goal is to get you as active as possible. The trails closest to the hippotherapy center are marked. We have all-terrain wheelchairs available, but they're not motorized. If you push yourself out on a trail, be sure you can get yourself back. Each chair is equipped with a GPS locator in case of an emergency. And don't worry, if you do get tired out there, we won't leave you stranded."

For a tiny thing, Abby had a strong presence. The complete opposite of the nurses in the hospital. They had tried to blend into their surroundings while Abby let you know who was in charge. "Can I trail ride?"

"Not alone. I promise you'll get plenty of saddle time to the point where you'll look forward to taking a break."

"I've spent my life on horseback. I don't think I could ever tire of it." Brady feared the facility severely underestimated his riding abilities.

"With all due respect, your body hasn't been through this level of trauma before, so don't be surprised if things don't feel the way they used to. Your injuries will limit what you can do at first. It's also my understanding you had a punctured lung and underwent six weeks of respiratory therapy."

Why did it always sound worse when somebody else said it? Not that he downplayed any of what had happened. It was the most painful experience of his life, but it was behind him. And that's where he wanted to leave it. She was beginning to remind him of Dr. Lindstrom.

"It's something your physician asked us to watch for," Abby added.

Of course she did. "What happens if I do need further respiratory therapy? Will you send me back to the hospital?"

"Not if we don't have to. We have other patients here that require it and we're capable of providing you with whatever you need." Brady wondered how long it would take to fully process that his hospital days were over. "In order to get on and off these horses, you'll need to learn how to maneuver up and down ramps," Abby continued. "I don't want to push your chair any more than I have to, just as I'm sure you don't want me pushing you. We'll focus some of our time today on teaching you how to get around, which you'll need regardless of how long you will or won't be in that chair."

Brady had woken up energized and now he felt exhausted before he'd even started. He exhaled slowly. "Where do we begin?"

Abby snickered. "If you're worried, then I've done my job. I want you to be hopeful, but not overzealous. I've heard stories about you, Superman." She handed him a helmet. "Try this on for size. Your therapy will be in multiple stages and we won't force you beyond what you're capable of handling. Where would you like your first lesson? Indoors or out?"

Brady turned his chair toward the door. "Out. I've been cooped up in a sterile hospital for over two months. I'm ready to get a little dusty and sweaty."

"Come on, cowboy."

After an hour of wheelchair exercises, Brady's arms felt like rubber and his head was on fire thanks to his helmet. But it felt good. It was hot, it was humid and it was pure heaven.

"Are you ready to try a horse?" Abby asked. "Or do you need a break?"

Brady shook his head. "I've never been more ready."

This was it. This was the moment he'd been waiting for. A team of six people approached him and a man named Thomas helped him up the ramp. Okay, so the ramp was more of a challenge than he had anticipated, but it didn't matter. He was about to mount a horse. He stood slowly, using the animal for support. The platform allowed him to easily slide onto the thin fabric saddle. His body began to shake and he wasn't sure if it was nerves, excitement, or if something was wrong. He gripped the horse's mane, relishing the feel of the coarse hair between his fingers. He closed his eyes and inhaled sharply. Each horse had its own unique scent and this one smelled like iced tea. He rocked forward in the saddle and felt a sharp twinge up his spine.

His eyes flew open. "What the hell?"

"Brady, tell me what you're feeling," Abby said.

"A—a sharp pain in my back." Brady sat frozen in the saddle, afraid to move.

His little team moved closer to him. "Can you lean back a bit and sit upright?" Abby asked. "We have you surrounded and I won't let you fall."

There was that phrase again, only he wished it was Dr. Lindstrom saying it instead of Abby. Yesterday her support had given him more strength than he realized he needed. He slowly rotated his hips backward and straightened his spine. No pain. "I'm good. It went away."

"Remember what I told you earlier," Abby said. "Your body's been through a lot and you need to give it a chance to reacclimate itself. That's why we're here. Ready for a walk around the arena?"

Brady gripped the handles on either side of the saddle. He instinctively searched for stirrups but there were none. He attempted to squeeze his thighs tighter around the horse's body as if he were riding bareback, only to realize he didn't have the strength. A hippotherapy team member closely flanked either side of him, while two people followed and two led the horse. He'd never felt more secure and more terrified at the same time.

The horse walked slowly around the outdoor arena. He'd never noticed the similarity between a horse's gait and a human's before. He'd read about it, but he hadn't fully understood it until now. As the horse's hips rose on one side, so did his own, forcing him to contract his core muscles.

Brady knew he had a goofy smile plastered across his face, but he didn't care. Today was the beginning of the rest of his life.

Chapter Three

It was the Fourth of July and Sheila had to work, just as she had every year of her residency. The only difference— she'd spend her afternoon at Dance of Hope and she'd see Brady Sawyer. The man hadn't been far from her mind since she'd discharged him four days earlier. She had tried to convince herself it was strictly out of concern for her patient, but even she didn't believe that story. He'd gotten under her skin in the most impossible way. She couldn't act on her attraction to him and she couldn't shake it either.

Sometimes an attraction to a patient was inevitable. But the feeling always disappeared as quickly as it came. Brady Sawyer had been out of sight for days, yet she found herself more excited than she should be to see him today. Marissa hadn't uttered another word about him. Then again, Sheila hadn't given her much of a chance. The busier she stayed, the sooner she'd forget about Brady.

By the time she pulled into Dance of Hope's parking lot, it was early afternoon. A small crowd had gathered near the Ride 'em High! Rodeo School outdoor arena. The summer students were competing in an informal exhibition and there was Brady Sawyer, standing at the fence watching the action.

Sheila had never understood why they'd built the rodeo school adjacent to the hippotherapy center. It just seemed to scream "look at me" to the hippotherapy patients. And then she looked at Brady hugging the fence rail—the poster child for "this could happen to you."

She redirected her attention to the patient files on the passenger seat. Flipping through them, she scanned the notes from last week's visit, then gathered her things and exited the car. Her focus immediately landed on Brady. Today he exuded pure masculinity, clad in faded denim jeans that managed to hug him in all the right places and a formfitting white T-shirt. *Good heavens.* She shouldn't care what the man wore. The fact that he'd been standing since she'd parked five minutes earlier should be her primary focus. His strength and stamina had clearly increased in a matter of days.

Sheila approached him. "You're not getting any ideas, are you?" Sheila asked. He turned toward her, almost toppling over. She knew better than to sneak up on him, but she had warned him she'd be watching.

"Dr. Lindstrom. This is a surprise."

"Didn't anyone tell you the rules?" Sheila detected the scent of Proraso aftershave. She knew the eucalyptus and menthol fragrance well. One of her fellow residents wore the same brand. She'd never cared much for it, but Brady's unique body chemistry transformed the fragrance from mildly annoying to downright tempting. "Everybody's on a first-name basis here. Please call me Sheila."

She noticed Brady's legs beginning to shake, but held her tongue. His chair was directly behind him and he'd use it when he was ready.

"You look nice." His admission caught her off guard, but it didn't seem to faze him. He eased into his chair and looked up at her, exposing more of his chiseled features to the sun. "I like you out of uniform with your hair down."

"Thank you." Sheila had almost forgotten that she'd changed before heading to the ranch. Scrubs were never worn outside the hospital. She'd chosen her best fitting jeans, lacy white top and red cowboy boots this morning after convincing herself it was patriotic and conveyed a professional yet casual appearance for her rounds at Dance of Hope. In reality, she chose the outfit because she knew she looked damn good in it and she wanted Brady to notice her. She had succeeded...now what?

"Are you checking up on me?" A slow smile spread across his face, forming a dimple in his right cheek.

"I'm checking up on all my patients. This is part of my residency program."

"Residency? You're not a doctor?"

Sheila winced at the question. It wasn't the first time someone had asked it, but it stung just the same. "I became a doctor the day I graduated from medical school. An orthopedic surgeon's residency is five years. This is my final year after which I'll become board certified. Then I'll begin my two-year fellowship in orthopedic trauma, providing Grace General accepts me in their program."

"I didn't mean to offend you." Brady shifted in his

chair. "I had no idea how the whole medical school and residency thing worked."

"No offense taken." Sheila wanted to ask about his education and what he'd do if competing was no longer an option, but feared she'd already crossed the forbidden doctor-patient line. "How are you feeling?"

"I've never felt sorer and more invigorated in my entire life." He leaned toward her. "I feel better already. Don't worry, Doc. I know I still have a long way to go."

"I noticed a difference when I pulled in. Studies have shown recovery occurs faster outside the hospital."

"Is that so?" There was that dimple again. He released the brake on his chair and motioned for her to follow him. "Do you have a few minutes to walk with me?"

Sheila checked her watch. "A few. What's on your mind?"

Brady turned onto the paved path alongside the hippotherapy center leading them away from the crowd. "I know you think my recovery is all about me, but I need you to know that I'm not doing this for selfish reasons."

Sheila stopped at a bench and sat down. "What I do or don't think shouldn't affect your recovery one way or the other."

"Alice told me the other day that I was selfish and using our son as an excuse to compete again and—"

"I'm sorry, who?" Sheila's heart stopped beating for a fraction of a second. *It shouldn't matter.* But it did. "You have a son? And a wife?" The last question left an awful taste in her mouth.

Brady shook his head. "I have a four-year-old son named Gunner, and Alice is his mother but we're not married. Never have been, never will be. I'm surprised you didn't know. They visited me at the hospital."

She probably would have noticed if she hadn't gone out of her way to avoid him during his stay. "I wasn't your physician then. I don't understand why you're telling me all of this."

"You may not have been my doctor, but I noticed you. It was impossible not to. A part of me secretly hoped you had noticed me too. I get it. There are many more patients than there are doctors and we become a number."

"You certainly weren't a number." Sheila took his hand and immediately regretted it when his other hand covered hers. Unwilling to let go, she braved a look into his eyes. "I'm probably one of the few people in your life who can honestly say they've seen inside of you." Sheila attempted a small bit of humor to derail the somersault of emotion cycling through her. "No patient is ever a number, at least not to me. I'm not trying to diminish who you are or your case in any way." She rose, pulling away from him. "What am I doing?"

"I'm sorry. I shouldn't have told you that."

"No, you shouldn't have." Sheila turned to face him, squaring her shoulders. "You do understand that nothing can ever happen between the two of us. It would cost me my job and I've already fielded questions about you. I don't mean to sound cold, but nobody is worth that sacrifice."

"Relax, Doc." Brady shrugged. "It was just a harmless flirtation. You're a beautiful woman, and I'm trying to get my bearings back. I didn't mean anything by it. It won't happen again."

"Good." His admission was oddly reassuring and uncomfortable at the same time. "Thank you, for saying I'm beautiful." Sheila knew she shouldn't have said anything but it had been so long since she'd heard a compliment she felt it deserved an acknowledgment. "I'm going to finish my rounds and then I will be back to see you because you're on my list too. So don't run off anywhere."

Brady pointed to his chair. "I don't think you have anything to worry about." They both laughed, easing the tension. "I'll be here when you're ready."

Sheila shouldn't have read anything into his reply, but the undercurrent had been undeniable. No man had ever had the ability to ruin her, but if she wasn't careful this one just might.

BRADY BARELY HAD time to recover from Sheila's rejection before he spotted Gunner dragging his grandfather up the walkway by the hand.

"Daddy!" Gunner jumped in his lap. "Easy, kiddo. Daddy's sore from all his physical therapy." His father reached over Gunner and gave Brady a hug. "It's good to see you, Dad."

"You look great," John Sawyer said. "You finally got some color back into you." The older man looked around. "This place is huge. I'm sorry I couldn't get here until today. Work has been crazy and this little guy has kept me busy."

"Once I'm on my feet, I'll pay you back with interest. I appreciate all you've done." He admired his father, but he hated the extra stress his accident had placed on the older man. He'd already had a heart attack two years ago and Brady didn't want him to risk another. His dad worked long hours on a residential construction crew in the hot Texas sun to help pay Brady's bills. It didn't matter how many times he or Alice told him not to, he picked up Brady's mail every day and paid whatever came in. Brady wasn't broke—yet. He had money in the bank, but every time he attempted to pay his father back, the man refused, telling him they'd settle up later. When Alice had the mail forwarded to her house, John called each utility and credit card company and sent them a check for the amount due. If anything happened to his father, he'd never forgive himself. That was one more reason he needed to regain his life.

John squeezed Brady's shoulder. "Eh, let's save all that nonsense for another time. Are you going to show me around this place or what?"

"I can show you, Pawpaw." Gunner climbed down from Brady's lap.

"You can!" John took hold of his grandson's hand. "You lead the way, then." He looked over his shoulder at Brady. "You coming, son?"

"I'll catch up with you. I left my phone back in the cottage. I want to get it in case Alice calls for him. I think Gunner wants to show you the rodeo school."

Brady watched them walk toward the corrals. His father and Sheila had missed each other by mere minutes. He'd barely composed himself after acting like a complete jackass before they'd arrived. He didn't have a clue what had compelled him to blurt out everything he'd said to Sheila. This was definitely one of those "in need of a do over" situations.

He wheeled down the path to his cottage. Despite all the things he'd said wrong, something Sheila had mentioned kept replaying in his head...she'd already fielded questions about him. When? And from who? He wanted to ask her, but he wasn't about to track her down and appear even more desperate.

After giving his father the grand tour, Brady was hot, sweaty and hungry. The hippotherapy center and rodeo school had a combined cookout to celebrate the holiday. Two hours had passed since he had last seen Sheila and he wondered if she'd left for the day without seeing him. He couldn't blame her if she had. Once they'd piled their plates with food and made their way to the picnic tables, Brady spotted her talking with Kay and a group of people he hadn't seen before. Then again, from his vantage point he seemed to miss quite a few things. He'd definitely developed a better appreciation for what it was like to be his son's height.

"I didn't want you to think I forgot about you." Sheila's voice almost caused him to choke on his hot dog. She patted him on the back a few times. "You okay? I didn't lose you in the hospital, I'm not going to lose you out here."

Brady cleared his throat. "I'm good. Dad, this is Dr. Sheila Lindstrom, one of my surgeons. Sheila this is my father, John, and my son, Gunner."

Sheila shook hands with John and readily welcomed a hug from Gunner. "Thank you for fixing my daddy."

Sheila cupped Gunner's chin and smiled. "You're welcome, honey, but I had lots of help." She turned to the table. "I hadn't realized how late it was. I didn't mean to interrupt your meal. Brady, do you have any questions or concerns for me?"

He had many questions and a few concerns, none of them relating to his health. "No, everything I'm feeling is muscle related. It's been a while since they've had this much of a workout."

"Dr. Lindstrom, why don't you join us?" his father asked. He attempted to shoot the man a look, but John refused to make eye contact, confirming to Brady he was up to no good. "Unless we're taking you away from your own family." *Subtle, Dad. Real subtle.*

"My family lives in Colorado. I'm not here with anyone."

"Then I insist." His father rose. "Have a seat next to me, I'll fix you a plate." Before Sheila could protest, John was halfway to the buffet table.

"Just for the record, I didn't put him up to that."

"I believe you." Sheila laughed. "He reminds me of my own father. Forgive me for asking, but your mom...?"

"She died shortly after Gunner was born."

"I'm sorry. That must've been really difficult, losing her at such an important time in your life."

"Thank you."

"Here you go." John set a plate twice the size of any of theirs in front of Sheila.

"My God, Dad. If she ate all of that she'd burst." His father was determined to embarrass him today.

"Oh, you'd be surprised what I could put away." Sheila thanked his father.

It was early evening by the time they finished eating. Gunner had dragged his grandfather off to the dessert table for seconds. "Thank you for humoring my dad. I don't want to keep you from your Fourth of July plans tonight."

"I rather enjoyed it. My only plans involve heading into town to watch the fireworks a little later. This is the first year I've been able to see them since I've moved here. I've always been on call. It's a rare night of freedom for me."

"Fireworks?" Gunner asked as he returned with an ice cream sundae in hand and a mouth full of whipped cream. "Can we come too?"

Brady didn't know if he should hug his son or reprimand him. He chose the middle-of-the-road approach. Wrapping his arm around Gunner's waist, he tugged him onto his lap. "If you want to see fireworks, ask Pawpaw if he'll drive us, but don't invite yourself to someone else's party."

"It's hardly a party. And you're more than welcome to join us. We're taking everyone from Dance of Hope and the rodeo school into town. You're a part of Dance of Hope, so you're automatically invited. That's what I was discussing earlier with Kay."

It wasn't the most private setting imaginable, but it was better than the alternative.

"We'd love to join you."

SHEILA HAD NO idea what had possessed her to offer Brady and his family a ride into town. After she had helped Kay pile all the kids into multiple ranch vehicles, she'd realized Brady was the odd man out. He hadn't been there long enough to form many friendships and she figured they'd look platonic enough with John as their chaperone.

With John and Gunner in the backseat of her car, she had to fend for herself up front with Brady. She'd never considered her Ford Fusion a small car, but Brady's hulking frame transformed it into a much more intimate space. Normally it wouldn't have fazed her, but after their little moment earlier followed by John's not-so-subtle matchmaking, her belly was flip-flopping like that of a teenager with a crush. Brady had crossed the invisible line between the seats more than once during their short drive into town. Accidentally, of course. That didn't stop her from enjoying the occasional arm brush.

All of Ramblewood had come out to see the pyro-technics. But the mayor had set aside a separate parking area for the Dance of Hope patients so they'd have an unobstructed view and not have to leave the vehicles if they didn't want to or weren't able to. The second Sheila cut the engine, John hopped out with Gunner in tow. So much for their chaperone.

Neither one of them made a move to exit the car. After sitting in silence for a good three minutes, Sheila opened the moonroof, and reclined her seat slightly. She had a comfortable front-row seat and didn't see the need to get out. Truth be told…she was quite content sitting in the dark with Brady by her side.

As the sky lit up in shades of red, white and blue, Brady reached for her. She didn't resist, enjoying the feel of his palm against the top of her hand. Their fingers entwined and for a few moments, they had what could never exist outside in the real world.

It felt good. So good, she knew she'd miss it tomorrow.

Chapter Four

Three days had passed since Brady had seen Sheila. In a way, it felt like only a few hours since he'd held her hand in the dark. But at times it felt as if it had happened years ago. Either way, he missed it more than he should. He hadn't even kissed the woman—not that the thought hadn't crossed his mind a few hundred times—and he was already craving her touch again. He'd held hands, kissed and done much more with his fair share of women and none of them had had anywhere near the same effect. Once he was capable of taking her on a proper date, he would plan a night she wouldn't forget. That is if he could convince her to say yes. He didn't want to endanger her job, but he couldn't stop thinking about her. Maybe they could find a way...

He wheeled his chair to the abdominal crunch machine in the fitness room and adjusted the weight plates to slightly more than he'd lifted yesterday. He'd been a little overconfident the first day, thinking he could crunch close to what he did preaccident only to discover just how much his ab muscles had atrophied in two and a half months. When he looked in the mirror, he still saw the same man he was before GhostMaker took him out…with the exception of numerous surgery scars. He could live with those. Rodeo cowboys and ranchers had plenty of them. And while they were still raw, they didn't bother him nearly as much as his lack of strength. Walking two feet without any assistance had become a daily goal he still couldn't master. *Weakness* wasn't part of his vocabulary.

He missed working on his house. He'd bought the small ranch thirty miles outside Ramblewood in January. Here it was July and he was already dipping into the money he'd set aside for renovations so he could pay the mortgage. He refused to allow his father to pay for his house. His dad didn't have the money either, but knowing him, he'd sure as heck try to earn it.

He longed to get back to the ranch and his career, but he missed playing with his son more than anything. Gunner's laughter was his favorite sound in the world. Now when his son looked at him, he saw worry in the boy's small face. No father wants to hear his child ask when he'll be able to play with them again. It broke his heart. Now that he was out of the hospital, they had the opportunity to spend more time together and have some long overdue fun.

Standing steadier every day since his arrival at Dance of Hope a week ago, Brady maneuvered into the machine's seat and slid his feet under the pads. He reached above his shoulders and firmly grabbed hold of the handles. He concentrated on contracting his abdominal muscles and slowly bent forward, lifting his thighs and knees toward his upper body, and then eased the machine back into position. By not allowing the weight plates to touch, he could keep constant tension on his muscles. With each set, his range of motion increased slightly. He'd probably be able to squeeze in only ten or fifteen reps before his physical therapist came in and scolded him for pushing himself too hard. They didn't understand. He'd continue to feel like half a man until he no longer needed anyone else's help to provide for his son.

Brady heard the door to the fitness room open. Choosing to ignore it, he closed his eyes and continued his workout. One or two more crunches meant one or two more steps away from his wheelchair.

"Ahem." A very feminine sounding throat cleared.

Determined to complete two sets, he refused to stop. Abby would physically have to block him this time. After another three crunches, Brady was surprised she still hadn't said a word. Grunting, he opened his eyes and saw two tiny red-and-black sneakers. His heart lifted. Slowly, he eased the weight plates down as his son eagerly danced in front of him.

"Surprise, Daddy!"

Brady unfastened his fingerless gloves and tugged them off. "Come here, little man." He slowly slid his feet out from under the pads and lifted his son into his arms. It was the first time since the accident that he'd held his son from somewhere other than a hospital bed or a wheelchair. It was a simple pleasure he wanted to enjoy for as long as he could. "I thought you were working today," Brady said to Alice.

"Rebecca wanted tonight off so we traded shifts.

Mom said she would watch Gunner. Since I had the day off, I thought we'd bring you your mail and see how you were doing."

"Be careful when you head home tonight." Brady hated when Alice worked the late shift at the emergency call center. Granted the police department was in the same building, but it wasn't located in the safest part of town. "How did you know where to find me?"

"The tiny blonde physical therapist said you sneak in here every morning when you think no one's looking."

So much for getting away with an unsupervised workout this morning. It was a nice move on Abby's part. She didn't have to put an end to his routine today. She'd had his son do it instead. That was okay... Gunner was a welcome interruption. "Mmm. What's that smell?" Brady sniffed the air.

"We brought you bre-fast, Daddy," Gunner said. "All your fav-rits. Show him, Mommy."

Alice held up a bag she had hidden behind her. "We stopped in town on the way here. Care to join us?"

Brady's stomach began to growl. "Most definitely." He eased Gunner onto his feet and gave him a playful poke so he would move out of the way. Alice reached for the boy's hand, leading him away from the equipment. While his son's back was still turned, Brady took the opportunity to stand and maneuver into his chair, consciously aware Alice was watching his every move.

"Wow," she said. "You're doing so much better than the last time I saw you."

Brady released the brake and grumbled a thanks before wheeling to the door. He was grateful for Alice and her support even though he knew how much she wanted him to retire from bull riding. As much as he respected her concerns, he wished his recovery hadn't come as such a surprise. He'd made it clear to her and anyone else who'd listen that he'd beat this. Alice hadn't quite grasped that concept yet.

They feasted on pancakes, sausage and eggs at one of the picnic tables facing the rolling hills of the Bridle Dance Ranch. The view from his ten-acre ranch paled in comparison but it was home and he missed it. Brady's father had taken his horses while he recuperated. That had been his father's choice of words. It made it sound so simple, as if he had the flu. But they both knew it would probably be months until he was able to care for them on his own again. Months was tolerable, forever wasn't. Despite his improvement, the more he spoke about getting back to his old life, the more people downplayed his career and told him either to take it easy or not to get his hopes up. Everyone except Gunner. Through Gunner's eyes, anything and everything was possible.

"You're thinking about home, aren't you?" Alice asked as she gathered their take-out containers and stuffed them into a paper sack. "You'll be there before you know it and then you can decide what you want to do next."

Brady wiped his mouth on a napkin before crumpling it. "I already know what I'm going to do next. So do you."

They watched Gunner waving to the horses near the corral fence. "I refuse to even entertain that idea.

You're out of the hospital and it's time for you to get your priorities straight."

"They are straight." Brady kept his voice down so Gunner wouldn't overhear them. "This is who I am, who I've always been. You've known me forever, know how much I love rodeo. I won't stop competing till I've won the World All-Around Champion Cowboy title at the National Finals Rodeo in Las Vegas. I can't possibly win this year, but just you watch—I will win. Until then, the money will pay the bills and keep me from losing my ranch."

"What about the fund-raiser your dad set up?" Alice asked.

Brady cringed. He'd been humiliated when he discovered his father had pleaded for donations on social media. His sponsors, family and friends had all chipped in, but it still wasn't close to the amount he needed. "I know Dad meant well, but I wish he hadn't done that."

"Are you mad that I contacted some of the relief funds designated to help injured rodeo competitors? Because if you are, you need to stop being modest and accept the help people are offering you."

"Those funds are meant for people with serious injuries."

"Brady, get it through your head." Alice grabbed his hands and squeezed. "I know you're feeling better and think you can take on the world, but this was a serious injury. You need to watch the video of your accident and see what happened to you."

Brady shook his head. He had refused to watch the footage the first ten times Alice had brought it up because he feared it would deter him from ever riding again. That was a fear he wasn't willing to face.

"Even with Dad's fund-raising, my health insurance and everything else, it still only amounts to a fraction of what I owe. It's not like I can get a second mortgage on my house. I don't have any equity in it yet. All I have is my job—my career. I need to be able to live—I need to be able to support Gunner. And even if money wasn't a factor, I'd still want to compete again."

Alice released his hands and waved him off dismissively. "Bull riding isn't an option and most likely it won't be ever again. Switch to one of the timed events, like roping or steer wrestling. At least it's safer. It terrifies me that this place is connected to a rodeo school. Haven't you heard one word the doctors have told you?"

"They don't know my body the way I do. I'm a bull rider. It's who I am. I need to compete in two events to qualify in the All-Around Cowboy category. That's where the money is. I've always competed in roughstock and I'm not changing now. Even if I wanted to, it's not like changing your shoes. We spend a lifetime training for our events." He raked his fingers through his hair, wishing he had his Stetson. He made a mental note to remind his father to bring it during his next visit. He felt vulnerable enough in his wheelchair—he hated feeling naked without his hat.

"I'd say they know your body better than you after all those surgeries," Alice hissed. "How many was it?"

"That's beside the point." Brady backed away from the table. "Thank you for breakfast, but I have to get to therapy."

For a moment, she appeared as if she might continue their argument. "I thought maybe Gunner and I could hang around here today. He really misses you, Brady. You're not in therapy all day, are you?"

"No, I'm not. I get numerous breaks throughout the day. I miss him too, but please do me a favor—keep him away from my physical therapy. I don't want him to see me like that."

"I don't understand what the big d—"

"I asked you nicely." Alice's relentless persistence was one of the many reasons why they weren't romantically involved. Everything was always an argument. "I want to spend time with Gunner and I'm fine with you staying the day, but please respect me enough to do this."

"Brady?" Sheila called out to him from the sidewalk leading to the picnic tables. "Is that your son climbing through the fence?"

Brady looked toward the corral and saw Gunner already had a leg and shoulder over the bottom rail. He stood to chase after him before his body had a chance to remind him otherwise. *Dammit!* He grabbed hold of the picnic table to prevent himself from falling completely forward. Sheila rushed to his side as Alice ran across the grass and pulled their son back through the fence. Gunner hadn't been in any imminent danger, but Brady's first instinct was to save him—and he couldn't. If Gunner got into trouble, he wouldn't be able to help him. That was unacceptable, and another reason to push himself.

"Are you all right?" Sheila asked, guiding him into his chair.

Brady attempted to shrug her off to no avail. *Great, now I have two persistent women in my life.* "I'm fine. Please let me do this on my own."

Sheila stepped to the side when Alice returned with Gunner. "He still doesn't understand that he can't pet every horse he sees." Gunner squirmed in her arms. "I'm Alice," she said to Sheila.

"I'm Dr. Lindstrom, but you can call me Sheila."

"I'd shake your hand but—" Alice struggled to keep a grip on Gunner. "He needs a nap."

"You can take him to my cottage," Brady ground out. "I'll come find you after hippotherapy."

"It was nice meeting you," Alice said to Sheila before carrying Gunner away.

He inhaled deeply. Sheila's scent hung like freshly laundered linens in the thick summer heat. He'd waited three days to gaze into her silver eyes, but now he couldn't look at her. Not after almost face-planting into the picnic table because he was too weak to chase after his son.

"I'm late for therapy," Brady said to Sheila, wheeling his chair onto the sidewalk.

"Do you feel pain anywhere?" Sheila walked alongside him. He appreciated her concern, but his embarrassment made him want to hide in his cottage with Gunner.

"Just my ego." Brady stopped at the entrance to the hippotherapy center. "The kindest thing you can do is walk away and give me a chance to regroup."

Brady didn't even have to look. He sensed when she stepped away. Confident she wouldn't follow him into the building, he pressed the automatic door button and wheeled into the cool corridor. As much as he preferred his hippotherapy outdoors, he wouldn't have to worry about Alice and Gunner watching him in the indoor arena. His therapy consisted of more than just riding horses. Walking and stair-climbing was a huge part of his morning routine and it could be excruciating. He wouldn't be able to concentrate with them there. It would serve only to reaffirm Alice's opinions on bull riding, and it might scare Gunner to see him in that kind of pain. No thank you. There were some things a man needed to do alone. This was one of them.

WELL, THAT WAS AWKWARD. Sheila hadn't expected to meet Gunner's mother this morning. She hadn't really given the woman much thought until she'd been face-to-face with her. She was attractive. She had huge blue eyes and glossy straight shoulder-length dark brown hair with bangs. Petite, but not short, she was one of those narrow women. Narrow hips, narrow shoulders. The type that made surgery more difficult because it didn't give her a lot of room to work with. She didn't hope to operate on Alice—it was just the way her brain worked 99 percent of the time. She was perpetually in work mode...unless she was in the dark with Brady.

The chances of that ever happening again were zero, zilch, zip, wasn't going to happen—couldn't happen—and she needed to eliminate all thoughts of it. Therein lay the problem. She couldn't get the idea out of her head. Even when she thought she had, he invaded her dreams.

Meeting Alice shouldn't have been awkward. Brady was her patient. She'd met many of her patients' family members. Was Alice part of Brady's family? She had to be something. They had a kid together. He said they weren't married, but that didn't mean she wasn't his ex-girlfriend or even his current girlfriend. Could Alice be his girlfriend? The thought alone made her uneasy. Patients fell for their doctors all the time. She'd dismissed Brady's attraction to her as a classic case of transference because she hadn't been his doctor all along. They had learned how to handle transference in medical school and this didn't fit. Nor should it matter.

That wasn't why she was there. She had two surgeries scheduled for the afternoon and had decided to make her rounds in the morning. Tomorrow hadn't looked promising either, and she didn't like going more than a few days without seeing her Dance of Hope patients.

In the rare event she couldn't make it, the facility employed two physician's assistants, ensuring the best care was available twenty-four hours a day should any of the resident therapy patients need it. The fellowship at Grace General ensured she'd continue her association with Dance of Hope—if she was accepted into the program.

Her first patient today was an army veteran who'd lost his leg after his Humvee ran over an IED pressure plate in Afghanistan. She wished Greg had half the fight in him that Brady had. At twenty years old, Greg had already faced the harsh realities of life. He didn't have a wife or child waiting for him at home. Despite months of mental and physical therapy, he still envisioned a future alone. It wasn't just his physical appearance. He feared he wouldn't be able to support a family. She hoped that eventually he'd realize he had the inner strength to overcome any obstacle.

It was close to noon when she finished her rounds. She had seen every patient except Brady. She popped her head into the physical therapy room just as he was taking his last few steps with the aid of the parallel bars. From her angle, she had a difficult time determining how much pressure he was putting on his legs and how much he was relying on upper body strength. She imagined the earlier incident at the picnic table helped propel him forward. If the pure grit etched on his face was any indication, he still had a lot of fight left in him.

She closed the door softly and exited the room unobserved. Sheila hated interrupting someone's physical therapy unless absolutely necessary. Patients deserved that time to focus on their recovery. Unfortunately, not all of her colleagues agreed. She'd seen countless doctors monopolize a patient's therapy time because they didn't want to inconvenience themselves. She had another hour before she had to be back at the hospital and didn't mind waiting.

Sheila wound her way to the community dining area. Meals were provided free of charge to all residents and staff, but Sheila always felt the need to put twenty dollars into the nonprofit's contribution box at the end of the buffet table.

She sat down at an empty table and unwrapped her

ham and cheese sandwich. After slathering it with mustard and mayonnaise, she tore open her bag of potato chips. She was stress eating and the chocolate peanut-butter brownie sitting next to her Dr Pepper confirmed it.

"Do you mind if we join you?" Alice asked. "I couldn't get Gunner to fall asleep. It's been impossible to settle him down ever since Brady left the hospital. He only wants his father."

"Please do." *Cue nerves.* She moved her bag aside to make room for them.

"We didn't really get to properly meet earlier." Alice held out her hand. "Again, I'm Alice. You said your name was Sheila, right? Are you Brady's doctor?"

Sheila shook Alice's hand. "You are correct on both accounts. I'm an orthopedic surgeon. I was in the OR the night he was admitted but only became his physician last week." She carefully chose her words, not knowing how much Gunner understood about his father's injuries.

"Has he discussed his future *intentions* with you?" Alice's emphasis didn't go unnoticed.

They both looked at Gunner who was happily munching on a chicken nugget while dipping his fingers in the barbecue sauce.

"He has," Sheila said. "I'm sorry, are you a family member? Because I can't legally discuss a patient without their permission." It was a legitimate question and one way of finding out more about Alice and Brady's relationship.

"Sort of. I mean, not legally." She ruffled Gunner's

hair. "We share Gunner and Brady's my best friend, but we're not together. I ask only because I hope—I pray— you are as strongly against his competing again as I am." Apprehension reflected in Alice's eyes. "He can't go back out there and I don't know how to get through to him. His father hasn't committed to the idea one way or the other, which shouldn't surprise me since Brady has a very singular focus, especially when it comes to bull riding. Unfortunately, those genes have already been passed down to my son and it's all he wants to do, even at his age. If there's any way you could sober Brady up to his new reality, I'd appreciate it. Gunner deserves to have a father who'll be around and be able to do things with him."

"I completely understand your concerns." Sheila wished she could reassure Alice further, but without Brady's consent or the knowledge of what Alice had already been told, she was very limited on how much she could say. "I have been well apprised of his career aspirations and I won't clear him for anything unless he's fully capable of handling it."

"Thank you."

Alice poked the lettuce in her salad with a fork before pushing it away as Sheila took a bite of her sandwich.

"I don't know if I should be scared or thrilled at the sight of you two together." Brady wheeled to their table, balancing his tray on his lap.

"Daddy!" Gunner climbed down from his chair and gave him a hug. "I missed you."

"You did! It's only been a few hours." Brady set his

tray on the table and lifted Gunner onto his lap. "But you know what? I bet I missed you more."

"No, I missed you more."

Brady wrapped his arms tightly around Gunner, burying his head in the child's neck. "Why do you smell like my aftershave?"

"You might notice your entire cottage smells like your aftershave," Alice said. "He saw it sitting there on the edge of the sink and decided he wanted to smell like Daddy."

"That's the downside to keeping everything at wheel-chair level." Brady set Gunner back down. "But it's only temporary, right Doc?"

"That's certainly our goal."

Sheila noted that Brady didn't seem too concerned she and Alice were eating lunch together. Maybe there really was nothing more to the relationship than Gunner. Then again, maybe he wasn't concerned because there was nothing more to his relationship with Sheila than a little flirting on the Fourth of July. After all, if Alice and Brady could have a baby together without a romantic entanglement, what was a little hand-holding? Nothing. And that's how it needed to stay.

"I'm just grabbing a quick bite to eat before I head to the hospital." Sheila debated wrapping up her sand-wich and stuffing it in her bag for later, then decided against it. She could handle another meal with him. "I had hoped to check in on you before I left, but I don't want to interrupt your family time."

Brady forked a piece of meat loaf. "You're not. I'm fine. I appreciate your checking up on me, though."

"Considering it's part of my job, it's not a problem." Sheila felt the need to restate her professional position to both her and Brady. "The next time I'm here, I do want to thoroughly examine you." Brady almost dropped his fork, causing her to immediately regret the statement. Alice's quiet giggle only reconfirmed how poor her phrasing had been. "I want to compare your mobility to last week."

"Just be gentle with me, Doc." Brady winked.

Alice sucked so hard on her straw it made a loud noise inside the aluminum can. "Oh! Sorry. Do continue." She beamed.

Was she actually condoning his flirtation?

"I'd like to talk to you before you leave." Brady's eyes held hers for a second longer than they should have before he looked at Alice. "Privately."

"I think he's trying to tell us something," she whispered to Gunner. "Can you at least let him finish his lunch?" she asked Brady.

"If it's nothing pressing, you have my number at the hospital and you can call me there. I need to be getting back anyway." Sheila stood and looked at the little family in front of her. They were cute together. She could see equal parts of Brady and Alice in their son. She admired their relationship, whatever it was. Maybe someday she'd have something similar, although she didn't know where she'd ever find the time or energy to provide the kind of attention a child deserved.

Seeing them together helped her understand Brady's desire to compete again even better than she thought she had earlier. She was beginning to see it wasn't just about money or being too proud to admit defeat. It was about taking pride in himself and his family. Gunner adored his father, in or out of a wheelchair. Hopefully Brady would realize he didn't have to be a champion bull rider to be a hero in Gunner's eyes. He already was one.

Chapter Five

Brady sat alone in his cottage, listening to the rain drum softly against the tin roof. The rain had started shortly after the three of them finished dinner. Alice had been right—his temporary residence smelled of his after-shave, but they'd decided to eat there anyway, wanting a little private time.

He would have preferred to see them to the car after dinner, but Alice had questioned if it was okay to get his wheelchair wet. He honestly didn't know. He didn't think water would cause any harm, but she insisted that he stay inside just to be safe.

Safe.

It wasn't her job to ensure his safety. It was his job to make sure his son and his son's mother were safe.

The majority of the day had felt more normal than he'd experienced in months. He'd eaten breakfast, lunch and dinner with his son. He and Alice shared custody of Gunner and he was used to having him around 50 percent of the time. Since they didn't have a formal court-ordered arrangement to adhere to, he saw his son whenever he wasn't traveling from one event to another. And Alice always made a point to join him when he competed locally. He'd spent a good portion of the morning doing hippotherapy and despite the borderline torturous physical therapy session he'd endured that afternoon, he'd begun to feel like his old self...until it came time for Alice and Gunner to leave and he couldn't accomplish the simple task of escorting them out.

He was mad. He was mad at GhostMaker. He was mad at himself for not holding on those eight seconds. He was mad for the miscalculation that had resulted in the bull goring him.

He was mad.

Brady closed his eyes and allowed the anger to fuel him. The angrier he was at the situation the more determined he became. He opened the bedside table drawer and removed an envelope Alice had given him earlier. If she had realized who it was from, he doubted he'd ever have seen it. The few sponsors that hadn't dropped him had donated substantial amounts toward his medical bills. It didn't come close to covering everything, but it definitely helped. When he'd opened the envelope earlier, he'd seen not only another check, but the rodeo schedule tucked neatly behind it.

He and his father had managed to keep the full extent of his injuries out of the media. The sponsors that had stuck with them fully expected him to compete again. He removed the schedule and clamped it between his teeth. He wheeled to the closet on the other side of the room and removed the folded walker Alice had noticed earlier when she and Gunner were playing hide-and-seek. When his father had placed Brady's empty suitcase in the closet last week, it had completely blocked his view of the walker. He locked it in the open position and extended the legs. After double-checking his wheelchair brake, he cautiously stood, gripping the tubular aluminum as if his life depended on it. If he was going to plan out next year's rodeo schedule, he was going to walk to the table and do it...not wheel there.

The chair Gunner had sat in at dinner was fewer than five feet away. His wrists and hands ached from his earlier physical therapy, but he refused to allow that to deter him. Inch by methodical inch, his arms and legs shook, rattling the walker. A few times, he questioned if it would support his six-foot-two-inch frame. With each step—regardless how small—Brady's heartbeat drummed in his chest. His body tingled, rejuvenated by the accomplishment. When he reached the hard wooden chair, he felt like a king sitting on his throne.

He carefully tore the picture Gunner had drawn for him earlier from the notepad and set it aside. He unfolded the schedule and reviewed the list, noticing it contained not only next year's dates, but this year's too. Was it possible to compete again this year? Even if it was just one competition, he'd take it. If he hoped to make it to the National Finals Rodeo in Las Vegas next December, he needed to get back in the ring sooner rather than later. Then he'd have a valid chance of winning some serious prize money. He'd just begun to hit his peak as a top competitor when the accident occurred. Most of the money he'd saved had gone toward his house and to pay down some of the debt he'd accumulated along the way. Winning the championship would more than support his son until his eighteenth birthday and possibly pay for college, providing he invested it wisely. Once Gunner's future was set, then he'd retire and get a normal job. Even if it was just mucking stalls, he'd be satisfied knowing he had provided for his son and made his mother proud.

She'd supported his passion until her final day on earth. When he was growing up, she'd made sacrifices in order to afford his entry fees. Her desire to see him win was as strong as his own. And in his heart, Brady knew she'd been his guardian angel the day of his accident. She was smiling down on him and he refused to disappoint her.

WHEN SHEILA LEFT the hospital, it was almost nine o'clock. After her two scheduled surgeries, she'd been part of the trauma team treating a three-year-old child who'd fallen off a second-story deck. It would be a miracle if he survived through the night. Some surgeries were more difficult than others, not because of the size of the patient, but because of their age and circumstance. The boy's spinal cord had sustained so much damage the neurosurgeon doubted he would walk again. Sheila still found it next to impossible to accept the cruel fate doled out to the unfortunate. And that's what they ultimately were. Unfortunate.

She arrived home too wound up to sleep. Her patient had reminded her of many of the children at Dance of Hope. They were at the hippotherapy center for various reasons. Some had cerebral palsy while others had lost limbs to bone cancer. Sheila had debated for two long years before she'd decided to specialize in orthopedic trauma surgery. As a level-one trauma center for both pediatrics and adults, Grace General provided the most advanced and comprehensive care available within seconds of a patient's arrival. Once Grace General accepted her into their fellowship program, her future would be set.

She'd lived only one other place in her life. Moving to Texas had been an adjustment, especially when she'd been forced to share a two-bedroom apartment with three other interns her first year. It had been all she could afford. Two years later, she'd moved into another shared apartment, but at least she'd had her own room. A few months ago, she had craved wide open spaces. Well, that and the rent was cheaper the farther she moved from town. The small house had rustic charm, a wraparound porch rivaling the main living area for square footage and a view of dairy cows across the street. Her life and career were headed in the right direction. So why did she feel so off balance?

Sheila trudged to the kitchen. Nothing relaxed her like baking sugar cookies. Between her and her mother, they'd perfected the recipe over the years. Her mother had been a high school English teacher and baking had been her way of unwinding after a particularly difficult day at work.

Sheila rummaged through her box of cookie cutters until she found a simple design she could easily decorate for both the pediatric wing at the hospital and Dance of Hope. She settled on a heart, knowing it would retain its shape without having to freeze the cutout cookies before baking as she usually did. Besides, who didn't love a heart? She'd decorate them in gender neutral colors and everyone would be happy.

It was almost three in the morning when her last batch of cookies came out of the oven. She'd already begun flooding the cooled ones with royal icing and then added names to the ones she intended to hand-deliver to her patients. Her hand froze when she piped out Brady's name on top of a bright red cookie.

"I did not just do that."

But she had. Brady's name sat on her kitchen table like a beacon glowing in the darkness. Out of the dozens of cookies laid out before her, Brady's stood out the most. Probably because it was the only red cookie with a name on it.

She wanted to phone a friend or ask for a lifeline. She was quickly losing her heart to a virtual stranger—a patient. It was commonly known as the Florence Nightingale effect. She'd never experienced it herself, but she'd witnessed other doctors and nurses succumb to it—some had permanently damaged their careers.

Sheila backed away from the cookie. She was too close to becoming board certified to risk anything on anyone. She covered the cookie with a paper towel, then picked it up and tossed it in the garbage can. Now if she could manage to toss away any romantic inclinations toward Brady she'd be set. Why was that so difficult?

BRADY AWOKE THE following morning hopeful—more than hopeful—now that he had a definitive schedule to work toward. The balance in his life that he'd lacked during the past few months had begun to return. His first thought that morning had been to call Sheila and tell her about his progress with the walker. Then he realized he didn't have her phone number. Why should he? She was his doctor, not his girlfriend. Calling and leaving a message at the hospital didn't have quite the same effect. It was all right. By the time he did see and speak to her again, he'd have progressed even further.

Besides, his father deserved the first phone call. The man had supported every one of Brady's hopes and dreams since he'd been a little boy. He'd never thought anything was out of Brady's reach. Where his mother had been more cautious and had always feared Brady would be injured in the arena, his father ignored the odds and the statistics, relying more on gut instinct. As much as he missed his mother, he was glad she hadn't been around to see him after his injury. It would have broken her heart to see her only child that close to death.

A shiver ran up Brady's spine. He admitted it—he had almost died. Alice would be thrilled to hear him say the words, and apparently so would Sheila after the lecture she'd given him in the hospital. He assumed with balance came clarity. Okay, he admitted it to himself. Now everyone would be happy and he could move on.

Brady had purposely left his wheelchair by the closet last night. He'd instituted a new rule before he went to bed...no more wheelchair while inside the cottage. It was small enough for him to get around without it. He needed to push himself if there was a possibility of his competing again this year.

Throwing off the bedsheets, he swung his legs over

the side. A deep, dull ache in his hips reminded him that he still had a lot of recovering to do. He wouldn't allow a little pain to scare him. It hadn't scared him yet.

Brady gripped the walker and slowly stood. By the time he reached the table a few steps later, he needed to sit down. He smiled at the picture Gunner had drawn yesterday. It was a stick figure with a hat on top of a large gray oval with horns. He ran his fingers over the image, the waxy crayon smooth to his touch. To his son, Brady was a bull rider. The rodeo was all he knew. He didn't have a college education or a trade to fall back on. He'd started mutton busting at Gunner's age and had kept his focus on winning the All-Around Cowboy championship in the years that followed. He wanted more for his son, which was why it was so important for him to win enough money to pay for Gunner's education. He wanted him to have options—options Brady hadn't had.

His last time on a bull could have been just that... his last time. Brady propped his elbows up on the table, rubbing his forehead. He stared down at Gunner's drawing. They'd kept telling him in the hospital that Ghost-Maker's horn had come within one inch of ending his life. One inch meant the difference between his son growing up with or without a father. The harsh reality was he didn't have any options. It was one thing wanting his son to follow in his footsteps and compete, but he wouldn't allow him to grow up without any skills outside the arena.

After calling his dad, Brady managed to get ready for therapy without using his wheelchair. It had been extremely slow going and he'd required numerous breaks, which had caused him to miss breakfast and his usual clandestine morning session at the fitness center, but his sense of accomplishment was even stronger than it had been his first day back on a horse. He quickly wheeled to hippotherapy, not wanting to keep his team waiting.

Brady was relieved to see Thomas when he entered the hippotherapy building. He respected the female therapists' abilities, but there were times when a man felt more comfortable talking with another man.

"I don't think I've seen you this happy before." Thomas greeted him with a firm handshake. "What did you do, have a hot date last night? I saw you with that brunette yesterday."

"Alice is just a friend." Brady checked over his shoulder to see if anyone was listening. "I do have a reason to celebrate, though."

After he finished telling Thomas about his progress with the walker, he fully expected another "don't overdo it" lecture. Instead, Thomas shook his hand again. "Congratulations. I knew you had it in you. Let Abby know when you see her later at physical therapy because we have wheelchairs that double as walkers. They still have big wheels to get you around, but they have rotating handles on top that allow you to configure them in multiple positions. You may not be ready for one today. But if you keep progressing the way you are, I can easily see you reaching that point very soon."

Brady's morning continued to improve. His hippotherapy session with Thomas and Thomas's wife, Gracie, was his best one yet. His body had begun to acclimate to the rhythms of the horse and all his different therapies combined. He knew what to expect with each session, even though they continually changed things up to work different muscles in his body. At Dance of Hope, his recovery was progressing at three times the speed it had in the hospital.

The only thing missing was someone to share it with. Before he could take his next breath, Sheila came to mind. He managed to push her out of his head while he did his therapy, but the second he stopped moving, the thought quickly returned.

"I don't want to be here," a young voice cried. "None of it matters. I'm just going to continue to get worse."

Brady wheeled his chair down the pathway alongside the hippotherapy center. A boy a few years older than Gunner argued with a man and woman Brady assumed were his parents.

"You haven't even given it a chance," the woman said.

"I don't want to. Please take me home." Tears streamed down the child's face, making Brady want to scoop him up into his arms and comfort him.

"Hey, hey," Brady soothed as he wheeled closer to them. "It's okay to be scared." Brady smiled up at the boy's parents, frustration etched on their faces. "I was scared on my first day too. But you know what? They take really good care of you here and help you in ways other places can't."

The boy stopped crying enough to look Brady up and down.

"My name is Brady. What's yours?"

"Ethan," the child squeaked out.

"It's very nice to meet you, Ethan." Brady wheeled a few inches closer to the boy. "Are these your parents?"

Ethan nodded his head.

"I'm Mary Fisher and this is my husband, William." She crouched beside her son's wheelchair. "See, honey, you've already made a friend." Mary attempted to smooth Ethan's hair but he dodged her hand. The pain of his rejection reflected in her eyes. "Ethan has multiple sclerosis. He was diagnosed when he was three, and this is his first flare-up in six months. It's also the first time he's needed a wheelchair. It's lasted a few weeks and his doctors feel hippotherapy will be very beneficial to him getting out of the chair."

"Why? I'm never going to be normal again."

Brady knew the feeling. "Can I tell you something?" Brady asked Ethan.

Ethan shrugged.

"After my accident, I wondered if I'd ever be normal again. I have a four-year-old son and I couldn't imagine not being able to do all the things other fathers and sons do together. And then I realized I had two choices. I could let my accident win and completely take over my life, or I could work really hard and hopefully get back to where I was. It wasn't easy, and even though I'm sitting in a wheelchair now, I was walking earlier today and I was walking last night. I had help with a walker, but I did it. And each day I do more. If I don't get back to normal, I'll just have to redefine normal."

"What happened to you?" Ethan asked.

"I had a little run-in with a bull."

Ethan's eyes grew wide. "Seriously?"

"I ride bulls and broncs for a living. It kind of goes with the territory." Brady didn't want to explain any further about his accident for fear the kid would equate falling off a bull with falling off a horse. "I'm doing much better now. And I think if you give this place a chance, you'll feel better too."

"I don't know." Ethan looked toward the corrals. "They look really big."

"Ethan's never been on a horse," William said. We don't live on a farm or a ranch. We live outside San Antonio and my wife and I both work in the city. This is new to all of us."

The fear in William's eyes matched his son's. Brady knew it well. Here was a father wanting to do what was best for his child—trusting in what others had told him was best. But William had just as much fear of the unknown as Ethan had.

"If it helps you any," Brady said to William. "I didn't know much about hippotherapy until a few weeks ago. I researched it and after reading everything I could find I made an educated decision to come to Dance of Hope. If my son were in the same position—knowing what I know now—I wouldn't hesitate to bring him here. New studies about the benefits of hippotherapy are conducted all the time."

"Thank you, that does help." William said.

"You must be Ethan Fisher," Kay said as she joined them. "And I see you have met our resident superman. Brady's improving more each day, just as I think you will too. Are you ready for a little tour?"

"Are we going to see horses?" Ethan asked.

"We can see them first if you'd like," Kay said.

Ethan shook his head wildly back and forth.

"Would you like me to go with you to see the horses, Ethan?" Brady asked. If he could offer any comfort to the child, he was willing to lend a hand. "I promise they're friendly." Brady turned to Kay. "I don't have another session until two o'clock. I'd be more than happy to tag along if that's okay."

"If it's all right with Ethan and Mr. and Mrs. Fisher, then it's fine with me."

Mary reached for her son only to be rejected once again. "Do you want Brady to come with us?"

Ethan nodded sheepishly.

"I'll be right beside you, champ," Brady reassured him.

"Do you want me to push you or can you do it yourself?" Kay asked.

"Oh, he can't wheel—"

Kay lightly touched Mary's forearm, interrupting her. "Ethan, what do you feel comfortable with?"

"I can do it myself." Ethan maneuvered his wheelchair alongside Brady's.

"William," Mary whispered. "He tires too quickly. It's too new to him."

"Then we'll be here to push him when he does. He needs to learn. Let him do it."

Brady understood and appreciated both sides of the situation. Ethan felt much the same way Brady had when he'd first started getting around in his wheelchair. He'd practically taken Sheila's head off when she'd pushed him without asking. In the same respect, he also understood the desire to do everything in your power to protect your child. His family had made similar adjustments for him the same way the Fishers needed to adjust to Ethan. Multiple sclerosis was foreign to Brady. When he got back to his cottage that night, he'd read more about it online. It was one thing for an adult to go through a life-changing event—it was altogether different for a child who had probably been running and playing with his friends days before to end up confined to a tiny seat on wheels. Half the time Brady couldn't understand what was happening to his body. He couldn't imagine how immense the confusion was for Ethan. It broke his heart. Children shouldn't have to suffer physically or emotionally. That was the belief that drove him. He wouldn't allow his son to suffer because of his mistakes. He'd recover to be there for Gunner, and if there was any way he could help in Ethan's recovery, he would do that too.

"THIS IS A SURPRISE," Gracie said as Sheila entered the Dance of Hope office carrying a platter full of heart-shaped cookies. "You baked! Oh, you shouldn't have."

"I was too wound up from work last night." Sheila set the cookies on the desk and gave her best friend a hug. "Besides, that makes up for the Fourth of July cookies I didn't have a chance to make."

"Are you here to see anyone in particular?" Gracie peeled back the plastic wrap and removed a cookie. "These smell insanely incredible." She took a bite. "Perfect as always."

"Why would you think I was here to see somebody particular?" Sheila wondered how anyone could possibly know she had a slight attraction—emphasis on slight—for Brady. She hadn't said anything to anyone.

"Pardon the lame cliché, but why do you look like you just got caught with your hand in the cookie jar?" Gracie narrowed her eyes. "What's going on?"

"Nothing is going on." Sheila snatched one of the cookies and popped the entire thing into her mouth, almost choking.

Gracie laughed, patting her on the back. "Are you all right? Here." She grabbed a bottle of water from the small office refrigerator, twisted off the cap and handed it to Sheila. "Drink this."

Sheila swallowed, embarrassed by her stupidity. "Thank you. That's what I get for eating so fast. I haven't had a chance to get dinner yet."

"I'm starved. Do you have time to grab a bite to eat or do you already have other plans?" Gracie asked.

"I'm free and I'm off for the rest of the night and tomorrow."

"Even better." Gracie handed Sheila the platter and grabbed her bag and keys. "I'm assuming the cookies are for everyone and not just me."

"I'll make you and Thomas your own special tray of cookies next week." Sheila followed her to the door.

"Let's drop these off in the cafeteria first," Gracie said. "We haven't had a night out in a long time, if you don't mind stopping by the house so I can shower quick and change. I look and smell horsey. Are you sure you didn't have any plans because you seem dressed to go out."

Sheila glanced down at her clothes. She'd chosen the outfit this morning knowing she'd stop by the ranch after work. She'd sorted through dozens of combinations before deciding on dark indigo jeans and a gauzy navy blue short-sleeved blouse with a white spaghetti strap tank top underneath. It was casual. It could even be considered business casual. Well, maybe minus the long gold chain and large pink quartz teardrop pendant. And maybe the gold bangles and long dangling earrings were a bit more than one would normally wear to the ranch to drop off cookies.

"Nope, I'm as free as they come." She didn't feel free. She felt desperate. Who else planned the perfect outfit just to drop off cookies at a place she'd visited a hundred times before.

"Do you feel up for Slater's Mill?"

"Slater's sounds great," Sheila said. No it didn't. She'd been on her feet most of the night before, making cookies and then all day at the hospital. The last thing she wanted to do was go to a honky-tonk to eat dinner and dance. She wanted to see Brady. She'd purposely stopped by at dinnertime so she could eat in the cafeteria. That plan had backfired.

She spotted him the moment they walked through the door. Brady was sitting at a table with another couple and a child in a wheelchair. His eyes met hers as she crossed the room. He lifted his chin in her direction and smiled. A megawatt smile that made her heart flutter as if she were a teenager at her first dance. She wanted to wave. But she didn't. She wanted to go over and say hello. But she didn't do that either. Instead, she stood in the center of the room with a tray of cookies in her hands, staring awkwardly at him.

"Are your feet glued to the floor?" Gracie asked.

"What? No, of course not." She took the cookies to the main buffet table and uncovered them. "Is that a new arrival sitting with Brady Sawyer?"

"Ethan Fisher. He came today—reluctantly. Brady has been wonderful with him. He's been by his side for most of the day."

"Really? Does Brady know them?" Sheila asked.

"No. According to Kay, Ethan is a city boy and was afraid of the horses along with being scared of his own prognosis. He has MS."

Another unfortunate child. "I hate to see that. I hate seeing it in adults, but it's even harder to see a child suffer with it. I read a paper the other day about the advances with hippotherapy and MS."

"There's Thomas." Gracie waved to her husband across the room. "Go over and say hello if you want. I'm just going to tell Thomas not to expect me until later."

"Why would I say hello to Brady?"

"I was talking about introducing yourself to Ethan and his family, but considering Brady is your patient that would be polite. What is with you tonight?"

"Nothing." Sheila rummaged through her bag for her phone. "You go talk to Thomas. I have to make a quick phone call."

"Your phone call will have to wait. Here comes Brady."

"Why is he coming over here?" Sheila dropped her bag on the floor and quickly bent to pick it up.

"You're jumpier than a long-tailed cat in a room full of rocking chairs." Gracie looked from Sheila to Brady and back. "No. You can't be. Are you involved with him?"

"No! Of course not." Sheila tugged at the bottom of her blouse.

"Mmm-hmm. Just be careful. I can't see the hospital looking too favorably upon that relationship," Gracie warned. "I'll be back in a minute.

Sheila contemplated making a run for the door, but she had a feeling Brady would be right behind her. The hallway had been empty when they entered the cafeteria a few minutes ago. It was much safer to talk to Brady in a room full of people than alone in the hallway.

"Hi," Sheila said.

"Hi yourself." Brady's slow Texas drawl made her warm all over. "You look very pretty. Hot date?" He winked.

"Gracie and I are heading into town for dinner."

"I wish I could join you."

"I wish you could too." The words flew out of her mouth before she even knew she was thinking them. "I—I mean. I—I'm sorry. I shouldn't have said that. I can't say that. Forget I said that." Sheila tapped her foot. How long did it take Gracie to tell her husband she was going out?

"I get to you, don't I?"

Sheila stared at him. "Wow. You've become very brazen overnight."

"Well, things have changed. You might not be my doctor for much longer."

"Why? Are you replacing me?" Sheila's fluttering heart now felt as if it was slamming into her rib cage.

"Nah." Brady reached out for her hands. Without even thinking, she took them as he slowly rose to stand before her. "As much as I love holding your hands, I feel confident enough to let go." Brady was less than a few inches from her. If she inhaled deep enough, her breasts would scrape the front of his shirt. She looked up at him, reveling in his masculinity. His broad shoulders made her want to rest her head against them and snuggle in the crook of his neck. "See, Doc. My legs are barely shaking. I've been waiting to show you."

Sheila quickly remembered where they were. She took a step back and scanned Brady's body. His legs were straight, his hips even, his shoulders back. He was right…there was very little movement in his legs.

"That's wonderful." Sheila smiled at the grand gesture he'd just made in front of the entire cafeteria. "How long are you able to stand?"

"A few minutes is my limit." Brady returned her smile and lowered himself into his chair. "I found a walker in my room and started using it yesterday, but I've been practicing my standing since I arrived at Dance of Hope."

"Maybe you won't need me much longer after all." Sheila was glad to see his recovery progressing. He deserved to move on with his life.

"I'll still need you, just not as my doctor."

Sheila jumped at the sound of Gracie clearing her throat behind her.

"I think you'll do just fine on your own, Mr. Saw-yer," Sheila said. "I'll check in on you during my next rounds. If you need anything, you can reach me at the hospital."

If Gracie was concerned about her relationship with Brady, she kept it to herself. Sheila knew it was wrong—so wrong—to love the way he'd just made her feel. Everyone wanted to feel needed. It was that much better when you heard the words. Brady would still need her. She'd allow herself to enjoy it, if only for a moment.

Chapter Six

Sheila had visited Dance of Hope five of the past eight days. It was perfectly normal. It was the middle of July, a few of her friends either lived or worked on the Bridle Dance Ranch and what better way to spend the summer than outdoors having fun? The hippotherapy center was on the ranch, so she found it perfectly acceptable to stop in and say hello to her patients. She hadn't had any in-depth conversations with Brady and there were days when she hadn't seen him at all. Okay...one day, but who was counting?

She was.

Sheila parked her car in Dance of Hope's lot. Cutting the engine, she rolled her shoulders in a weak attempt to banish the stress she'd created for herself. She'd turned into one of those people she despised. She ran into them frequently at the hospital. A nurse who went out of her way to run into a doctor she lusted after. A friend with a secret crush who found every excuse under the sun to drop by a patient's room to bring them something they might need. And then there were the girlfriends and boyfriends of new interns who didn't quite understand that their significant others' long hours were due to their jobs and not an affair. Yep, she'd become an *excuser*, as they were commonly referred to at the hospital. And she'd found her own excuse to visit.

Excusers were the butt of jokes and Sheila could officially add her name to the list. She tried telling herself that it was all right since she'd managed to keep her conversations with Brady strictly professional. She asked him how he was feeling, double-checked his progress with his physical therapists and moved on to the next patient. Maybe she didn't factor in watching him from afar or catching him watching her out of the corner of her eye, but looking never hurt anyone. As long as she wasn't caught.

She stepped out of the car. This afternoon, Sheila had legitimate appointments at Dance of Hope. Brady was on her list—the bottom of the list. The reports she'd received from all of his therapists reiterated his desire to compete again. She admired his drive and determination, knowing he'd continue to push his body to the limit. Every bone, every muscle, every ligament had a breaking point and she feared Brady would push himself past that point.

Sheila checked her watch. It was a little past one. She had a few hours to complete her rounds before she would chastise herself for staying longer than necessary just to spend time with the man she couldn't have. After swinging by the main office, she made her way to the outdoor hippotherapy corrals.

In under a second, Sheila zeroed in on Brady…form-fitting jeans and all. He was standing and leaning—

not bracing himself against, but leaning—on the fence rails. She scanned the area behind him for his wheelchair and noticed it had been replaced with a combo walker-wheelchair. A grammar-school-aged girl rode by on her hippotherapy horse. Each time she passed, Brady waved his hat in the air and cheered her on. The hat was new. Sexy too.

"He's wonderful with children." Kay Langtry gave her a welcoming hug.

"I've noticed him offering support to a few people this past week."

"It's so much more than that," Kay said. "He has a way of relaxing our new residents, especially those who haven't been on a horse before. He sat with the parents of one child for a long time last week, reassuring them he would bring his own child here if the need ever arose. In fact, his little Gunner has made friends with quite a few of our hippotherapy children. I wish Brady wasn't so gung ho to get back on top of a bull again. I'd hate to see something happen to him."

Brady slowly made his way to the corral gate with the aid of his walker as the young rider dismounted with assistance from her therapists. She hobbled to Brady on crutches, stopping to give him a high five before continuing to her parents. This was why Sheila had become a physician—to improve people's quality of life. Nonprofits like Dance of Hope did the same. And then there was Brady. An extraordinary team had put him back together and he planned to risk it all as soon as she gave him the all clear.

Even knowing what he planned to do once he left

Dance of Hope, watching him with the children made her warm and fuzzy all over. Sheila wasn't a warm-and-fuzzy person. She cut into people and put them back together for a living. She was a blood-and-guts person. *Warm* and *fuzzy* weren't even part of her vocabulary, yet Brady turned her insides to mush every time he looked at her.

"Am I detecting a crush on our Mr. Sawyer?" Kay nudged her playfully.

Sheila fought a smile, but her lips betrayed her. She could deny it all she wanted to everybody under the sun, but she found it impossible to fib to Kay Langtry.

"It's not that simple," Sheila began. "It's one thing to admire him from afar, but I can never act on it. He might be tempting, but he's off-limits."

"What if he wasn't?" Kay asked.

She'd asked herself that same question many times. "I can't answer a hypothetical question like that. I'm a scientist—I rely on facts and figures. Besides, it doesn't matter. Even if he weren't my patient any longer, the hospital would consider any personal involvement with Brady an ethics violation. They're pretty strict about those things. It opens them up to lawsuits. I'm not going to risk my career for him."

"I've seen the way he watches you. I'd say the feelings were mutual."

Sheila knew they were. He had subtly—and not so subtly—implied his feelings a few times. "That's not helping, Kay. It's complicated."

"It shouldn't be. We can't help who we fall in love with."

Love? Who said anything about love? "We definitely have not fallen in love with one another. You can't fall in love with somebody you don't know. And we're virtual strangers. Although, every day I come here I seem to learn something new about him."

"I've noticed you have been coming around much more frequently," Kay persisted. "We used to see you once a week. Now you're here every other day, sometimes two or three days in a row. That didn't happen before Brady came along."

"I have friends here." That was the truth.

"Yes, and you're always welcome." Kay squeezed Sheila's hand. "But I haven't seen you visit your friends this much before."

"What are you trying to tell me?" Sheila wasn't sure she even wanted Kay to answer.

"I'm not trying to tell you anything, dear. Far be it for me to get involved in your affairs—I mean business."

"Oh no, you would never do that." Sheila wrapped an arm around Kay's shoulder.

"Sometimes we're presented with a once-in-a-lifetime opportunity." Kay walked with her. "Taking it may drastically change your life. Not exploring the opportunity can have an equal if not more detrimental effect. Just something to chew on."

Chew on? "That's a whole lot of thought for one mouthful," Sheila said.

"I don't want to keep you from your rounds. If I don't see you before you leave, have a wonderful night." Kay ducked through the back door of the hippotherapy indoor arena, her matchmaking mission complete for the day.

"You too," Sheila called after her, but the door had already closed.

She began to smooth the front of her shirt when she realized she'd done it again. Although she tried to tell herself otherwise, every outfit she picked out was for Brady. But it shouldn't be. He—they—couldn't be. She was marching down the sidewalk in the direction of the physical therapy room when she heard her name. She inhaled sharply at the sound of his voice, but continued to walk. She felt his presence close behind her and since she knew it wasn't a medical emergency, she needed to keep walking for sanity's sake.

"Sheila!" The sound of the soft tires of his wheelchair rolled up behind her. He had the speed advantage. "Sheila, wait up."

She spun to face him. "Mr. Sawyer, you're interrupting my rounds."

"I'm one of your patients, see me first." He beamed.

"That's a bit forward of you." True, but still forward. "If I see you now, I won't come back and see you later."

"Yes you will." He lifted his chin in defiance.

"Excuse me?" Now he was a bit too presumptuous, despite the dimples that deepened as his smile grew. *I will not be swayed by dimples.*

"You've been avoiding me all week."

"No I haven't. I've said hello and we've had a conversation or two."

"A passing 'hello, how are you?' does not constitute

a conversation," Brady said. "You're my doctor. You're supposed to give me the utmost care."

"That's right, Mr. Sawyer. I'm your doctor."

Brady's eyes widened as he no doubt realized he had just backed himself into a corner. "So that means we can't be friends?"

Sheila pursed her lips, debating how to answer. It was an honest question. Maybe not so innocent, but it was definitely honest. And it deserved an answer. "In my profession it's very difficult for a doctor to befriend a patient. Especially a patient of the opposite sex. I'm not saying it's not done, I'm saying it's difficult."

"Nothing worth having is ever easy," Brady countered.

"I wouldn't say that. If I won a new car, it would definitely be worth having."

"I like your car." Brady glanced behind him and then leaned forward. "It has a very cozy front seat."

Sheila felt the heat rush to her cheeks. Blushing was a trait she'd left behind in grade school. Now she was warm and fuzzy and blushing. *Wonderful.*

"Moving on," Sheila warned. "You look different. More cowboy, less patient. You've come further than I had anticipated you would at this point. I like the hat."

"My dad had a chance to stop by yesterday and bring me some things from my house. I needed to feel more like me. I've always worn a hat and have felt naked without it." Brady tilted his brim back a little more, exposing his insanely gorgeous blue-gray eyes. "Sweats and track pants may be comfortable, but a cowboy needs his jeans." Brady laughed. "I can get through most of my day, including hippotherapy in these. I just change when I have physical therapy. Once I can get my cowboy boots on and off, then I'll be satisfied."

Sheila glanced down at his well-worn sneakers, suspecting he'd had them since his high school gym days.

"I got a new ride too." Brady stood—cautiously, but with relative ease. He walked to the back of his chair, each step methodical yet surefooted. "I can flip the seat forward and rotate the handles allowing me to use it as a walker. If I get tired, I can sit down and wheel around like I can with a normal wheelchair."

"Kay told me she was getting these in." After all the research Sheila had conducted on physical therapy and patient recovery, she was astonished more facilities didn't use the chair. "It's the first time I've seen one in person."

"I can't even begin to explain how amazing it is to walk again." Brady's face radiated excitement. "I'm trying to do it as much as possible. Now that I'm not restricted to walking only in my PT sessions, I feel invigorated."

It was hard not to share in his jubilation. She wanted to. He deserved to be happy, but she wouldn't be doing her job if she wasn't at least a little cautious. She wished all her patients were as fearless and determined as he was. A few weeks ago, she had seriously doubted he'd return to bull riding. Watching him stand before her now, she acknowledged it was possible.

"I would like you to come in for follow-up testing. It's been just over two weeks and your body has been through quite a lot. I'd like to run some scans and make sure you're continuing to heal properly."

"Sure thing. When do you want me?" It was a simple question, but Sheila detected desire behind the words and it wasn't necessarily unwanted desire, despite her principles.

"I will see what I have available when I get to the hospital tomorrow. Until we get your test results back, I want you to ease up on your physical therapy."

Brady's smile slid from his face. "Why? I'm not feeling any pain. I feel wonderful."

"You should never lie to your doctor. I get reports from all your therapists and I know much of your PT is painful."

"I power through it." Brady sat down and released the hand brakes. "You're going to tell Abby to back off my therapy, aren't you? That's fine. I can continue to do the same therapy in my cottage. You can't stop me. It's bad enough I get this crap from Alice, but not my own doctor. I have faith in your abilities, why can't you have faith in mine?" Brady spun his chair around.

Sheila had taken an oath to tread with care in matters of life and death, and that care extended beyond the operating table. She might not be able to act on her feelings for Brady, but she'd do whatever it took to protect him from himself. Even if that meant he'd hate her for it.

BRADY RESENTED SHEILA summoning him to the hospital. It had been three long days since he'd last seen her. She'd stopped coming around the ranch as frequently. And that suited him just fine.

That wasn't true. He missed her angelic face. He wanted to explain why this meant so much to him. He wanted to make her understand. He wanted to kiss her, dammit.

Brady spent much of the morning either being poked and prodded or in a doughnut-shaped machine getting a full-body CT scan. Due to all the metal in his body, MRIs were no longer an option. He still hadn't seen Sheila, but he'd met with four nurses, a neurologist, a radiologist and two employees from the finance department.

Brady had scanned the checks he'd received from his sponsors into the mobile banking app on his phone. Thank heavens for technology. Combined with the money his father had deposited from fund-raisers, Brady was able to write the hospital a large enough check to pacify them...momentarily. Of course, they wanted more and he had more, but he needed to set money aside for his son. He had no idea when he would collect another paycheck and he refused to give all of what he had away.

After his CT scan, he wheeled down to the cafeteria. He was finally allowed to eat something other than the dye he'd had to drink earlier. Maybe he should be nervous, but he wasn't. If he didn't like what Sheila had to say, he could always get another doctor. He knew his body. He would never push himself to the point where he couldn't perform. He was determined, not stupid.

After settling on pork medallions and sweet potatoes, Brady realized he didn't have much of an appetite. He twisted open a bottle of water and took a long swallow. The radiologist had told him Sheila would call him with the results, but he'd insisted on staying in the hospital and waiting. She'd forced him to come in and he was going to get his results today.

Frustrated, Brady pushed away from the table. He stood, reversed the handles on his chair and plodded to the hospital atrium. The open space seemed different than it had the last time he'd been there—with Sheila. Only an hour of his two and a half months in the hospital had been spent with her, yet the first memories that popped into his head were of Sheila.

"Brady?" It took him a moment to realize she was actually beside him and not just invading his thoughts.

He turned to face her. "Dr. Lindstrom."

"I understand you would like your test results today."

He turned his palms upright and shrugged. "Did you honestly expect anything different? It's already been three days since you told Dance of Hope to ease up on my therapy. You're setting my progress back every day. I'm not waiting any longer."

"I should hear from the radiologist shortly. If you would like to follow me, I can complete your exam. I won't have the results of your blood work today, but we don't need them to continue your physical therapy."

Brady attempted to keep pace with her. "Are you in a hurry?"

Sheila jammed her hands in the pockets of her white lab coat. "No, I'm not. I'm sorry." She waited for him to catch up. "How many steps are you taking a day?" Sheila motioned to the black band around his left wrist.

"I didn't notice you wearing a step counter the other day."

"I ordered it online and had it shipped overnight to Dance of Hope." Brady stopped walking and sat in his chair. He tapped the device lightly, smiling at the display. "I told you I wasn't going to give up."

Sheila placed a hand on his shoulder. "I never want you to give up. I don't want any patient to give up." Her touch seared through his shirt. He'd craved it for days and immediately missed it when she withdrew. "I just don't want you to push yourself so far that you set yourself back. That's why you're here." She continued walking. "If Dr. Mangone felt you didn't need any further treatment, he would've released you to Dance of Hope and that would have been it. We're here—I'm here—to ensure you make the most complete recovery possible. Believe it or not, I do have faith in you."

Hearing her say the words meant more to him than it should have. She didn't sound like a doctor talking to her patient. She sounded more like a wife talking to her husband. Brady inwardly laughed at the thought. *Marriage?* Someday he wanted to settle down and have more kids, but that was way in the future. Years in the future. Well, maybe not too far. He was almost thirty after all.

Thirty-five was a great age to get married. Then he could have his next kid at thirty-six. He'd have retired from bull riding by that point, and hopefully have cleared his debt and set aside enough money for Gunner's future to be able to focus on having more children and finding a stable job. Doing what, he still didn't know. But the more time he spent watching the kids at the rodeo school, the more he began to entertain the idea of one day becoming an instructor. He'd need more wins before he reached that point. No one wanted to learn how to ride from a wannabe champion. Recognition went a long way in the industry.

Of course, none of these plans meant anything until he was fully recovered.

"Brady, where you going?"

He stopped wheeling and looked around. Sheila was ten paces behind him, standing outside an exam room door. He'd been so deep in thought he hadn't realized she'd stopped.

"Sorry." Brady returned to her side and wheeled through the door. "My mind was elsewhere."

"I'm going to give you a few minutes to change into this." Sheila handed him a hospital gown. "And then I will be back to wrap up your exam."

It was hospital gown number three that day. He should start a business creating more manly hospital patient attire. He tugged his shirt up over his head. Numerous scars crisscrossed his chest and abdomen. He slid his track pants to the floor and stepped out of them. More scars peeked out from underneath his boxer briefs, a long one trailing down his left thigh. They were red and ugly. He still hadn't seen himself in a full-length mirror. They were conspicuously absent from Dance of Hope. There was a small mirror above the sink, wheelchair height, and he could see some of his scars in it, but not all of them.

For the first time in his life, Brady actually felt insecure about his physical appearance. He slipped into the gown and sat down in his chair. He'd always taken his body for granted. He was fit and athletic. He certainly never minded a woman seeing him naked. Here he was, half-dressed in a hospital room and he felt more vulnerable than ever.

"This is crazy." Sheila had seen him in a hospital gown before. He hadn't had a Texas-size crush on her then, though. She knew his scars—she'd helped close the wounds that had created those scars. Brady ran his fingers along the one on his leg. It was raised and smooth, completely void of body hair. He'd gone out of his way to flirt with the pretty doctor like a complete fool. Many male patients had probably acted the exact same way. The connection he'd sworn they had was laughable when he thought about it.

A nurse followed Sheila into the exam room and closed the door behind them. "I just phoned radiology. We should have your CT results within the hour. In the meantime, you still haven't answered my earlier question. How many steps are you taking a day?"

After another brief lecture on overdoing physical therapy, Sheila notated each and every one of his incisions. Her hand had covered almost every inch of his body as she checked each bone, every joint. He'd never thought a woman touching him would feel so cold and so impersonal. He'd dreamed of Sheila touching him again, of touching her. Instead, he felt like a lab rat.

"That'll be all, thank you," Sheila said, dismissing the nurse. "Just let me know when those results are in."

"There are a few things I'd like to discuss with you.

Do you want me to give you a moment to get dressed?" Sheila asked.

Hell, he'd come this far. What difference would it make if he changed in front of her? "Nope, you've seen it already." Brady shrugged out of his gown, and tugged on his pants before Sheila had a chance to turn away. "Don't keep me in suspense, Doc." Brady slid his arms into his T-shirt, then slipped it over his head. "As far as I can tell I passed all your tests."

"We're still waiting on some of your results, but I'm certain your blood work will come back fine."

"As will my CT scan," Brady said through clenched teeth. He wanted to get his clearance from Sheila so he could get back to Dance of Hope and squeeze in a physical therapy session today. He'd left his watch at the cottage and had no idea what time it was. He didn't want to pull out his phone for fear he'd appear even ruder than he felt at the moment.

"Brady, you're a remarkable man." Sheila sat on a blue vinyl-covered stool across from him. "And you're right, I'm sure your CT scan will confirm that your recovery is progressing nicely. That doesn't guarantee 100 percent recovery. You're back on your feet, you have goals you're working toward every day and, yes, I will most likely sign off on your physical therapy today." She moved the stool closer to him. "But I'd be remiss if I didn't talk to you about the real possibility of not competing again. Not because I don't want you to—not because Alice doesn't want you to—but because you may not be able to. That's a very possible reality and I don't feel you have taken it seriously enough."

"Wow!" Brady's knee bounced up and down. "One minute you're praising me—the next minute you're cutting me down."

"That's not at all what I'm doing." Sheila stiffened her spine.

"You told me you had faith in me before, now you don't."

"It has nothing to do with faith. It has to do with the body's ability to heal. I have more experience with this than you do. And in my experience, I don't believe your body will be able to compete again. I don't want to give you false hope. I also don't want you to give up."

"You don't?" *What the hell?* The woman was confusing him.

"Of course not. I don't know any doctor who wants their patient to give up." She started to reach for him then quickly retreated. "I want you to be the very best you can possibly be. And if you recover enough to compete again, then more power to you. But no, I don't want to see you on the back of a bull." She rested her hand over her heart. "I don't want you back in this hospital again as my patient. I don't want to read about you in the newspaper."

She exhaled slowly, leaving Brady to wonder which one of them was more anxious. "In my professional opinion, from what I'm seeing when you move and when you walk, the tightness in your joints, the lack of flexibility in your hips, I just don't see you competing again, even with physical therapy. My advice is to talk to somebody about it. I can recommend a great therap—"

"A psychiatrist? You want me to see a psychiatrist?" Brady shoved his feet into his sneakers and yanked his cell phone out of his pocket. He dialed Dance of Hope. "I'm not a head case." Kay Langtry answered on the second ring. "Hi, it's Brady. I'm ready to leave the hospital. Would you be able to send the transport to pick me up?" He hung up. He had twenty minutes to wait, and it certainly wouldn't be anywhere near Sheila. "Would you please give me something in writing that I can bring back to Abby so I can continue my physical therapy?"

"I wasn't talking about a psychiatrist." Sheila removed a pad from the drawer and scribbled out a note. "I was talking about a transitional therapist. They help patients reacclimate after life-changing injuries." She tore the page off the pad and thrust it into his hands. "I can help you only if you're willing to help yourself."

"I don't need the kind of help you're offering. Goodbye, Dr. Lindstrom."

Chapter Seven

Sheila waited until Monday to give Brady the results of the rest of his tests. She'd felt he needed the weekend to cool off after he'd stormed out of the hospital on Friday. The results wouldn't have deterred him anyway, so she hadn't seen any harm in waiting.

She'd had Sunday off from the hospital and had chosen to do nothing at all. She had one guilty pleasure at home. The pink-and-purple nylon hammock she'd purchased during her first year of college. The thing stuffed into its own rucksack and weighed a little over a pound. Whenever she went on vacation, which was a rarity these days, she brought it along. She'd slept in it on numerous camping trips, hung suspended over streams and watching eagles soar while relaxing on the slope of a snow-covered mountain. She called it her thinking pod and yesterday she'd needed some serious thinking time. She'd hung it between two trees in her backyard and swayed in the shade for the majority of the day.

She stood outside Brady's cottage, uncertain if she should knock or just leave the test results along with the cookies she'd made for him. She lifted her hand to knock and thought the better of it. Apologies weren't exactly her forte—clean breaks were. *Turn and walk away.*

She knocked.

No answer.

She knocked again.

She sealed the manila envelope containing the test results and set them along with the cookies on his doorstep. As she straightened, Brady answered the door, barefoot, with the aid of an aluminum cane. His dark hair was tousled and wet, a simple white T-shirt clung to his still-damp skin, and his well-worn faded jeans—*good heavens*—hugged his hips and thighs like nobody's business. The undone top button exposed a hint of flesh and left Sheila wondering if he wore anything beneath.

Stupid, stupid, stupid. She shouldn't have knocked.

"I come in peace." She picked up the envelope and cookies and handed them to him. "Did I catch you in the shower?"

"I was just getting out when I heard you knock. I still don't move very fast." Brady held up the clear cellophane bag and inspected the contents. "I don't believe I've ever seen cookies decorated as white flags before."

Sheila attempted a smile and felt awkward. Really geeky awkward. She didn't know what to say. She was a physician, skilled in the art of breaking news—both good and bad—to people in various states of distress. Yet she couldn't find the words to talk to Brady. Instead, she stared at the bottom of his frayed jeans. Even his toes looked sexy.

She tucked her hair behind both ears and braved a glance. Brady stood watching her, his head tilted slightly as if trying to read her innermost thoughts. Swallowing hard, she clasped her hands and then unclasped them, suddenly unsure what to do with them. She opted to slide them into her back pockets, and the movement thrust her breasts in his direction. *Crap!* Folding her arms across her chest, she grinned up at him.

"Yeah, um. So, those are your test results."

"You could have called or emailed them to me." Brady tore open the envelope and flipped through the documents.

This wasn't going as expected. "You're right." The thought had crossed her mind. "I didn't like how we left things on Friday. I fear I overstepped as your physician."

Brady stepped away from the door. "Would you like to come in?"

Don't do it, Sheila. "Sure, thank you."

The immediate intimacy of the small residence set off a million warning bells in her head. That and the fact that his bed was fewer than twenty feet away.

"Have a seat." Brady motioned to the couch in front of a bank of windows. He set the cookies on the coffee table and joined her. "Where are my manners? Would you like some coffee or Coke?"

"No thank you, I can't stay long." She shouldn't be alone behind closed doors with him. "I wanted to see if you had any questions about your results. I must admit, I'm surprised to see you getting around with just a cane."

"I've been using it for a couple of days. Only when I'm indoors and near places where I can readily sit down." Brady reached under the table and raised it with a simple touch of his finger. "I need to get one of these for my house. It's perfect for Gunner's little projects."

Sheila immediately regretted her decision to come inside. His close proximity was too casual, too tempting, too everything. She studied his profile as he read the cover sheet. Evening stubble shadowed his jawline. She fought every urge to reach out and touch it.

"Help me out here, Doc." Brady's brows furrowed. "If I'm reading this correctly, you're telling me everything's fine?"

Sheila nodded. "I even consulted with Dr. Mangone and he agreed. We couldn't have asked for better results."

Brady dropped the report on the table and pulled her into his arms. His calloused hand guided her face to his as their lips met. Her brain urged her to push him away, but her body smothered any lingering logic. She wanted this—she wanted him. His fingers snaked into her hair drawing her closer, deepening their kiss. The tip of his tongue skimmed hers, playfully at first, then more demanding. Her hand trailed up his thigh, pausing just below his hip. Brady grabbed her wrist and tugged her across his lap until she was sitting astride him. He held her face between his hands and stared into her eyes.

"I can't tell you how long I've wanted this." Brady's slow kiss left her body thrumming like a masterfully played instrument. He was gentle and firm at the same time. His hands, strong and powerful, skimmed over her shoulders with the lightest of touches, creating multiple shivers along her spine. He leaned forward, kissing the base of her throat. She tilted her head back, gripping his muscular upper arms. He was forbidden and she wanted to taste more of him.

"We can't do this." *Was that me?* Sheila barely recognized her own heady voice.

"Don't you want me?" he whispered against her lips. "I used to watch you at the hospital and wonder what it would be like to kiss you."

Sheila groaned. "Don't tell me that." Her euphoric fog began to clear when he mentioned the hospital. "Brady." She pushed against his shoulders. "We can't do this."

She slid off his lap, embarrassed she'd let it go as far as it had. She'd never crossed that line with a patient before. It wasn't real. His feelings for her were nothing more than relief and excitement about his test results. He'd been right. She could've phoned or emailed them and she knew better than to put herself in this position.

"Can you honestly deny your feelings for me?" He entwined his fingers with hers, urging her toward him.

Sheila stood, backing away from the couch. "That doesn't matter. We both need to forget these feelings exist." She shouldn't even have feelings to take into consideration. But she did. She'd wanted that kiss just as much if not more than he did. If they were any two other people on earth, she'd kiss him again. *No, no, no.* She was his doctor. He was her patient—her younger patient. Okay, so she was only older by two years, but still... "This is wrong."

"You want me just as much as I want you." Brady leaned back, draping his arms over the back of the couch. His cocksure smile both warmed and irritated her. "And I'm not talking about sex. I'm referring to the whole package. That's why you're so dead set against me competing again, isn't it? My body's showing you I can do it, but you keep trying to convince me otherwise."

He was insightful, she'd give him that. She'd pretty much come to the same realization yesterday. She'd wished they had pictures or video of Brady when he'd first arrived in the OR so she could show him how close to death he'd looked, how torn up. Maybe that would scare him enough to keep him from getting back on a bull. It terrified her to think of him being in that condition ever again. That thought screamed ethics violation. She cared. She cared more than she had a right to. Cared more than she even wanted to.

"This can't happen again." Sheila squared her shoulders. "It happened, we got it out of our systems, we don't mention it to each other or anyone else. I could lose my job over that kiss, and I'm sorry, Brady, you're not worth my career."

"Then, you're fired."

"I'm what?" Sheila threw her head back and laughed heartily. "You can't fire me as your physician, Brady."

"Actually, I can." It wasn't the optimal choice, but if it meant having a chance with her, then he was fine with it. "You're telling me it's an issue because you're my doctor. If I eliminate the problem, then we can date."

"It's not that simple," Sheila said.

"Sure it is." Brady leaned forward, resting his elbows on his knees. "Unless you're not really attracted to me." He'd already laid his heart on the line. He needed to know one way or the other how she felt about him.

Sheila's smile tightened. "I think we've already established my attraction to you and vice versa. Grace General Hospital frowns on doctors dating former patients. I'd lose the respect of my colleagues. And if you run to my attending and have me removed as your doctor, it will raise a few red flags."

"We'll give them your white flags in exchange." Brady held up the bag. Mutual attraction shouldn't come with a lead weight attached to it. It should be light and fun. He wanted the chance to experience that excitement with her, but she had to lighten up a little.

"Nice. Real mature." Sheila scowled. "You just confirmed why we can't be together." She strode to the door and opened it, then changed her mind and slammed it shut again. "Any man in my life would have to respect my career. You don't have a clue what physicians sacrifice. I put my entire life on hold to become a doctor. After eight years in school and another four in Grace General's residency program with another year to complete before I begin my fellowship, I'm not throwing it away for a fling. Dedication and devotion from people like me is the reason you're alive today."

"Sheila." He hadn't meant to upset her. "I do respect your career. I admire your dedication and achievements." If she only understood that he'd devoted the same energy to his own career.

She scoffed. "You take everything for granted."

Brady stood and reached for his cane. "Wait just a minute. I admit I don't get the whole ethics violation thing and I'm sorry I teased you about your job." She'd managed to rile him as if he were a bobcat with a burr under its tail, and he wouldn't tolerate it. "But insinuating I take my life for granted is not acceptable. You don't know me."

"You are so hardheaded." She stepped toward him. "And I can say that with 100 percent certainty. I helped give you a second chance at life. A second chance to see your son grow up and you want to throw it all away for pride."

"I'm doing this for my son," he argued. "Why can't you see that?"

"Gunner doesn't care what you do for a living. He's four! He loves you no matter what." Sheila threw her hands in the air. "Okay, I'm done with this conversation. I don't care what you do." Sheila reached for the doorknob and hesitated. She slammed her fist into her thigh. "So help me, I do care." She spun to face him. "That's the problem. I care what happens to you. This speech is nothing new to you, is it? You've compared me to Alice before. I'm sure she's said the exact same things I'm saying. It doesn't matter. You'll do what Brady Sawyer wants to do."

Brady hadn't expected Sheila to admit her feelings for him. He'd suspected and even hoped the attraction was mutual. Hearing the words gave it a completely different meaning. How could he walk away from a woman who intrigued him like no other?

"It's not pride." Brady walked to the bedside table and opened the drawer. Removing a stack of paperwork, he brought it to the table. "Humor me for a minute." He spread out the numerous hospital bills, pointing to the grand total at the bottom of each. "You don't come cheap."

Sheila picked up one of the invoices and perused the items, before picking up another.

"Have you ever even seen a bill from your hospital?"

Sheila sat down at the table. "Not as extensive as these." She continued to pick through the papers. "You weren't a typical emergency room case."

"It doesn't change the fact I have to earn a living to support my son." Brady sat beside her. "Gunner is everything to me. Without him, I'm nothing. He came into my life at a very, very difficult time and he's a blessing like no other. I refuse to allow him to go without."

"I know you want to be a good father." Sheila gathered the bills and stacked them neatly. "There are other ways to support your son."

Brady rested his hand on her forearm. "I admire your dedication to your career. I admire your education. I wish I had a fraction of it." He held his arms out wide. "This is it. This is me. This is all I know how to be—a bull rider. A rodeo cowboy."

"You're so much more than that," Sheila whispered.

Brady laughed and rubbed the stubble along his jawline with his palm. "My father devoted all his spare time to make me a champion. He sacrificed everything. Both of my parents did. And I failed—miserably. I made a mistake and it almost cost me my life. Growing up, I spent every day after school honing my riding skills. We didn't have schools like the one next door. We learned from other cowboys. As I got older I devoted every weekend—every free moment—to being the best competitor. When the season was over, I worked odd jobs here and there. Nothing permanent. Once the season started up again, I was back on the road. Everything I earned went to the next entry fee and my travel expenses." Brady carried the paperwork back to the drawer. "When Gunner came along, I had to choose my events more wisely. Higher entry fees meant higher payouts. And I was good. I made a solid living at it. Hell, I haven't even owned my ranch for a year yet and I might lose it because I can't pay the bills."

"What about Alice? And your dad?"

Brady shook his head "Alice is a great mom, but she can't do it all alone. She shouldn't have to. My dad's giving her money right now. Do you have any idea what it's like for a man to have his dad pay for his son? It's demeaning. I feel like a castrated bull."

Brady raked his hand through his hair. If he was going to let Sheila into his heart, she needed to know—to understand—what drove him to compete again. "I love what I do and I am grateful for the support my family has given me through years. But it kills me that you and everyone else close to me want me to give up. There's too much at stake and it's not all about money. My mom might still be alive if I hadn't competed that weekend. She'd planned to go with us, but she hadn't felt well the previous night. Dad wanted to stay home, take care of her. But she'd have no part of it, said she'd probably just caught a bug." Brady closed his eyes, still able to hear her voice in his head. "She told me to win for her, and I did. When we got home we found her in bed. She'd suffered a massive stroke and died alone."

Brady felt Sheila's warm touch against his cheek. "It wasn't your fault." He opened his eyes and met her gaze. He entwined his fingers in hers, knowing they were partially responsible for him being alive today.

"It sure felt that way. I know my father still questions his decision to leave that day. He'll never admit it. Hell, he won't even talk about her. I have to live with wondering what would have happened if I had insisted he stay home. My mom made the ultimate sacrifice so I could compete with my dad by my side. She wanted me to win and not just that day. It was important to her that I follow my dreams and succeed. And I will. I refuse to let her down."

"I didn't realize."

"Now you do." Brady gave her hands a gentle squeeze, urging her to stand. He brushed the hair from her face and lightly caressed her cheek, relishing the feel of her skin beneath his fingertips. The desire to take her to his bed and make love to her until she understood almost overrode his senses. "Can't you give us a try? I'll wait. You've already said I'm improving and you won't need to be my doctor for much longer. There are other orthopedists not associated with the hospital I can see if I have a problem."

Her eyes welled with tears. "It's not just that. I can't

give my heart to someone knowing every time he goes to work may be the last time he leaves home whole."

Brady released her hand. "How is this any different from other professions? Look at deep-sea fishermen and lumberjacks. Aren't those the most dangerous jobs in the world?"

"That's a job—this is a sport," Sheila argued.

"A professional sport, like football and racecar driving," he countered. "It's called being a professional rodeo cowboy for a reason. I hate to break it to you, but my so-called sport is a job. Asking me to walk away from that is like asking you to walk away from being a physician. The only difference is I know I'll have to walk away from my job within the next few years. Retirement comes early for us. It's a short-lived career, but make no mistake, it is a career."

"I understand where you're coming from and I sympathize with your reasons, but I'm saving lives and you're risking yours. This goes against everything I believe in."

He made his way to the door and opened it. "Then I guess we have nothing more to discuss."

Sheila dropped her head. "No, I guess we don't."

Closing the door behind her should have been easier. It shouldn't hurt. He understood her not wanting to jeopardize her career. After all, he wasn't willing to give up his career for anyone either. Including her.

SHEILA LEANED AGAINST the side of his cottage for five minutes before she willed her feet to move. She had to walk away. She'd made the right decision. *Then why did it feel so wrong?*

Brady's door clicked open. She scurried around the corner in an attempt to hide from him. Seeing her still there would serve only to strengthen his argument. A child's bloodcurdling scream came from the cottage next door. Before she could react, Brady flew down his front ramp. Unable to support himself completely without his walker or cane, he fell to the pavement onto his knees.

"Brady!" Sheila ran to his side. "Don't move."

Brady shifted his legs into a sitting position. "I'm fine."

"Are you sure?" She offered her hand as he attempted to stand.

"Forget about me, will you. Go check on the kid." Sheila jumped back at his harsh tone. She ran up the ramp next door and pounded on the door. "This is Dr. Lindstrom, are you all right in there?" She tried the knob—locked. She pounded again. "Please, open the door."

A crowd had begun to gather around the cottage. Thomas made his way to the door with a master key card in his hand. Within seconds, they were inside. A terrified preteen girl had her wheelchair backed into a corner while an enflamed frying pan burned on the stove. Thomas quickly grabbed the extinguisher, and put out the blaze.

"Oh my!" The girl's mother ran into the cottage. "What happened?"

Sheila checked the girl for burns. "Just a little kitchen fire. She appears to be okay. Scared, but okay."

"I'm sorry," the girl cried. "I wanted to make my mom dinner for all she's done for me. I know how hard this is on her."

"Oh sweetheart." The woman knelt before her daughter, wrapping the child up in her arms. "Shh, I'm here."

"I'll send Housekeeping over to clean up the kitchen. They'll bring you a fresh fire extinguisher and a new frying pan," Thomas said.

Relieved, Sheila followed him out. When she returned to Brady's cottage, he was gone. She had a hunch where he might be. A few minutes later, she found him in the fitness room working the parallel bars with Abby by his side. While she further understood his determination, his relentless fight to push himself to the limits worried her. Something had to give and she feared it would be Brady before too long.

Chapter Eight

That kiss. That earth-shattering kiss. She wanted to tell Gracie. Heck, she wanted to scream it from the hospital rooftop. It was a secret she couldn't share. Her lips had still tingled when she'd awoken that morning. Disappointingly, she hadn't dreamed about him last night as she'd anticipated. The only way she'd ever have Brady was in her dreams.

Sheila stood outside Dr. Mangone's office knowing full well she should report the kiss and step down as his doctor. The kiss, at least the extent of the kiss, had been equally her fault. Even Sheila had to admit Brady's offer to wait and find another doctor had been moderately appealing. All right, it had been downright tempting, but not worth the professional backlash that would ensue.

She couldn't risk her career over a man—not again.

But, she realized now, even if she'd been a florist instead of a physician, she wouldn't date Brady. Love was too rare and too precious to lose in an arena. She'd seen the devastated families of those who'd risked too much and died before their time. That life wasn't for her.

Sheila walked away from Dr. Mangone's door—she wasn't going to get involved with Brady and there was no point in damaging her reputation over a kiss. She'd become one of those women who were married to their career. Maybe she'd adopt a cat or two. At least she'd have somebody to come home to.

Her pager went off, as did several others around her. Mass trauma en route. Sheila ran for the elevator and pressed the button repeatedly.

"Hurry up, hurry up."

The doors opened as she and seven other trauma team members entered. She closed her eyes, clearing her mind of all things, including Brady. The image of his lifeless body filled her vision. Her eyes shot open. Not now. Not ever. The elevator door slid open again. It was showtime.

BRADY WALKED STEADILY down the sidewalk to the rodeo school's outdoor arena with the aid of a walker. About a week had passed since he'd kissed Sheila and he still hadn't seen her. An office building had collapsed and she'd been working mandatory overtime. At least according to a resident named Marissa that Sheila had sent twice to make her rounds.

He shouldn't even want to see her after the way they'd ended things last week. He'd offered her a chance—a solution—and it wasn't enough.

"Hey, son, how are you feeling today?" John Sawyer slapped him on the shoulder.

"This is a surprise. I'm doing great, Pops." Brady

gave his father a hug. "I'm barely using the chair any-more."

"Before you know it, you'll be back home."

Brady noticed his father said home and not *bull riding* as he had during his entire hospital stay. It was especially odd considering a bull riding session was going on fifty feet in front of them. "You've been talking to Alice, haven't you?"

John shrugged. "I talk to Alice every day."

"Pops, come on." He hated when his dad played coy.

"I was hoping to bring Gunner by after I got off work today, but Alice wanted to take him to the county fair tonight."

"She couldn't wait another day? The fair runs for two weeks." Brady hadn't seen Alice either. His father had brought Gunner by once during the past week and his son's absence had begun to worry Brady. "Why isn't she letting me see him?"

"You're jumping to conclusions. They still serving dinner in there?" John nodded toward Dance of Hope. "I'm starving."

"Me too." Brady turned his walker-wheelchair around just as they released a bull and rider from the chute. He stopped and watched the young cowboy execute a perfect eight second ride and dismount. *God, I miss that.*

Now a few paces ahead, Brady's father waited for him to catch up. "I know you're worried about seeing Gunner. You have to understand, every day is the same here for you. But it's summer. Gunner's little playmates have invited him on day trips and to swimming pool parties. The kid has a pretty full schedule."

"And I'm missing it." Kids grew up so fast and by the time he left Dance of Hope, he'd have essentially missed four months of his son's life. That was a lot at Gunner's age.

"You could be missing a lot more," John said.

"What's that supposed to mean?" Brady already knew the answer.

"Nothing."

For the first time Brady noticed his father's more-salt-than-pepper hair and slumped shoulders. The man had aged rapidly and Brady had an idea when it had begun. He couldn't remember his father looking so weathered before the accident. He'd been by Brady's side the entire time. Now his father had to work twice as hard to support not only himself, but also Brady and Gunner.

"What aren't you telling me?"

"I don't know, son." His father removed his hat as they entered Dance of Hope. "The more I think about you getting back on a bull, the less I like it."

"So Alice has gotten to you."

John shook his head. "No. No she hasn't."

"Then it was my doctor."

"You mean that pretty thing you were fawning all over? I wish she would call on me. She was cute." John elbowed Brady mockingly. "I haven't spoken with her either. I may be getting on in years, but I can still form my own opinions and I've done some research on that internet you're so fond of. Before you say anything, hear me out, son. I know I can get you a job working with me."

"You honestly want me to quit—to give up everything you've taught me." Brady never imagined his father joining the antirodeo task force.

"I hope I taught you how to be a father more than I've taught you how to compete." John gripped him by the shoulders. "A part of me wonders if you're looking for the easy way out—a fast cash grab to pay off your debt. Life doesn't work like that. So what if it takes you ten years to pay off your hospital bills, hell it may even take you twenty. At least you'll be around for those twenty."

"I'm doing it for mom too."

His father took a step back. "Aw shucks, I didn't want to do this with you today."

"But you were planning to do it." Brady wondered how long his father had felt this way. Had he been pacifying him all this time because he didn't think he'd be able to compete again, only to finally come to the realization it was a real possibility? He thought he knew his father better than that. Then again, he thought he knew a lot of things he didn't.

"I had to tell you how I felt. That's the kind of man I am. I'm also the kind of man who stands beside his son no matter what. If you decide to compete again, I will support you, but as your father, I wish you wouldn't. I know I don't say it enough, but I love you, son."

"Pops, I love you too." Brady gave him a hug.

"And your mama loves you, God bless her. Come on, let's get us some supper and you can tell me more about that pretty doctor you've been pining for."

It was the first time his father had openly mentioned his mother. It wasn't much, but it would do for now. "I have not been pining for Sheila," Brady said under his breath.

"Don't lie to me." John waggled his finger in Brady's face. "I raised you. I know what you look like when you're thinking about the rodeo and I know what you look like when you're pining over a woman. You had your pining face on when I pulled up."

Brady laughed loudly. "Pops, what am I going to do with you?"

"Stick around long enough, and maybe you'll figure it out." John entered the cafeteria, leaving Brady to stand in the hallway, the laughter gone.

Now he didn't know what to do.

SHEILA LOVED SURGERY but she missed her routine more. She walked through Dance of Hope's main entrance, pausing to stop at the photo of the man behind the hippotherapy center's vision. She'd never met Joe Langtry personally, but she admired his strength and commitment to the community. The fact he was astride a bucking bronco in the photograph didn't help matters when it came to Brady Sawyer. If he could only see past the snapshot he had of himself, he would develop his own vision for the future. She trailed her fingers along the picture frame and smiled at Joe. "Maybe you're the answer I've been looking for."

Sheila made a beeline for Kay Langtry's office. Unable to find her, she scoured the grounds until Gracie informed her Kay had gone into town to meet some friends for dinner. Sheila wanted to find out if her idea was worth pursuing without raising Gracie's suspicions. Kissing Brady had heightened her anxiety over being caught. She tried to tell herself if she found Brady an alternate source of income that was both acceptable and gratifying to him, then she'd be able to walk away... or it would give her another reason to consider a relationship with him. No, dating a patient—current or former—was off-limits. Her intentions were purely unselfish. Weren't they?

She hadn't purposely avoided him for the past week but she had welcomed the much-needed break. She left the rest of the world outside when she entered the operating room...at least she used to. Every time she operated on another man from the horrific building collapse, she saw Brady lying on her table. And that was one of the many reasons doctors shouldn't get involved with patients.

During her internship she'd been warned by her attending to never get involved in a patient's personal life. Especially when it came to family members and their ability to pay. She'd followed that rule to the letter except when she was concerned for her patients' safety. Her inquiries had uncovered a handful of abuse situations. She always feared abuse when broken bones couldn't be explained, especially among children and the elderly.

"I need your opinion on something," Sheila said to Gracie.

"Sure." Gracie attached lead ropes to two of the hippotherapy horses. "Do me a favor. Can you bring those two in behind me?"

Sheila snapped lead ropes on the remaining two horses and followed Gracie into the stables.

"Do you see any future potential for Brady to work here, at Dance of Hope?" Sheila asked.

"Thomas and I were talking about that the other night." Gracie took the ropes from Sheila and led each horse into its stall. "He'd make a great therapist. He's supportive, driven and goal oriented, but he'd never do it. You're paid a pretty meager salary the first year while you're earning your certification. Is that what you wanted to talk to Kay about?"

Sheila followed Gracie back outside to collect the rest of the hippotherapy gear. "I thought maybe if it came from Kay he might consider it."

"I guess it's worth a shot, but he's determined to compete again." Gracie collected the helmets and fabric saddles from the fence rails. "That's his daily motivation. He doesn't say much to me about it, but Thomas says it's pretty much all he talks about. Plus he's already begun training with Shane over at the rodeo school."

"Wait. He's training with Shane Langtry?" Sheila blew out a breath. Shane wasn't just one of the school's owners, he was renowned for turning riders into champions.

"He started working him a few days ago. Honestly, if he was going to train with anyone, Shane's the best he could have asked for. He won't push Brady past what he's capable of handling. May I ask why you're taking such an interest his personal life?"

Sheila wanted to argue that she was just inquiring into a patient's well-being, but she feared Gracie would become even more suspicious. She opted to go with the truth. At least part of the truth. "After you've put a patient back together, it's difficult to watch them return to the activity that caused the original injury. Those are the ones we tend to keep a closer watch over."

"Fair enough."

"Are you and Thomas free tonight?" Sheila asked. "It's mandatory I take the next two days off and it's probably my only chance to go to the county fair this year."

"That sounds good. Do you want to ride out there together?" Gracie asked.

"I came here straight from the hospital, so I'd like to go home and shower first. Do you think we could meet up around seven at the main entrance?"

"Sure, let me feed the horses and find my husband before he makes other plans. He's been playing poker with some of our older residents. Brady's the ringleader."

"Uh-oh, I heard my name." Brady appeared out of nowhere on the path. "Good to see you, Doc. You just missed my dad. He was asking about you. What was this about me being a ringleader?"

"I was talking about your poker nights. You have fleeced my husband out of three bags of pretzel sticks already." Gracie folded her arms across her chest. "Have you no shame?"

"Nope." Brady winked. "Your husband bets with

those honey mustard pretzels. They're worth more than regular pretzels."

"Yeah, well. You're just going to have to make do without him tonight. He's my date for the evening." Gracie lightly brushed Sheila's arm. "I'll meet you at the fairgrounds entrance at seven. And you behave yourself, Brady. I don't want to hear about any more people going into pretzel debt."

"Will do, ma'am." Brady touched the brim of his hat. "Heading to the Luna County Fair tonight? Alice took Gunner there this afternoon. You look great by the way."

Sheila reached up and attempted to smooth her messy ponytail. She'd been so frazzled when she'd left the hospital she hadn't even dared a glance in the mirror. She'd planned on avoiding Brady this evening since Marissa had given her a full progress report the day before.

"You're just being polite, but that's okay. I'll take any compliment I can get today." Sheila scanned the length of his body, noting he'd replaced the chair walker with a regular aluminum one. While she was glad to see his progress, she'd have felt better if he was using one of the walkers with a built-in seat just in case he needed a break. "You look even better than the last time I saw you."

Sheila closed her eyes and hung her head. She couldn't believe she'd just implied he'd looked good the last time she saw him. He had, in all his after-shower prekiss glory. *Oh God, that kiss.* "I should be—I need to get going. I have to shower and change before I meet up with Gracie and Thomas later."

"Thank you for that vision."

"What? What vis— Oh!" Great, now she could add babbling to her warm, fuzzy, blushing list. "When I last saw you, you were mad at me. Now here you are picturing me in the shower? How does that work?"

"I'm a guy."

"Alrighty then." Sheila had hoped he had a better answer, but the guy excuse was for the best. If he had said something sweet and charming, she'd probably swoon. Then she'd have to add that to the list too.

"I have missed you and I apologize for yelling at you when I fell."

"That's forgotten. I understood where you were coming from," she lied. The day had been on her mind since she'd last seen him. Not because she was mad, but because she'd witnessed how strong his desire to help others was—and in an emergency, he couldn't.

"One thing that bothered me, though." Brady took a step closer to her and lowered his voice. "Why were you still outside my cottage so long after I'd asked you to leave?"

Sheila closed her eyes and shook her head slowly. "I will not answer that question."

"Okay." Brady stepped away from her. "Have fun tonight, I wish I could join you. I could use a little fun."

Sheila watched his retreating form. She felt guilty for not asking him to join them. Technically, he could have. But if anyone from the hospital saw them together—it was too risky. She'd mention it to Thomas, then maybe he could arrange an outing with Dance of Hope tomorrow. That would be acceptable. Anything more than that was crossing the line and Sheila didn't know if she'd be able to stop herself the next time.

"ARE YOU SURE you can get yourself back to Dance of Hope tonight?"

"I got it covered, thank you." Brady had hitched a ride to the county fair with the brother of the resident army veteran, Greg.

"I wish I could have gotten you closer to the gate."

Brady expanded his aluminum walker and tested it on the hard-packed dirt. "I'm good. I'll consider it part of my therapy." He waved goodbye and trudged toward the fairgrounds entrance. By the time he made it there, it was half past seven. His body was drenched in sweat and his shirt was clinging to his chest. Not exactly the romantic image he wanted to portray. His arms and legs ached. It had been one thing walking around Dance of Hope and Bridle Dance Ranch—trekking half a mile across the parking lot was unexpected.

He paid his entry fee and hobbled to the nearest vendor. He desperately needed water and a place to sit. Calliope music played in the background as bells rang from impossible-to-win carnival games. He twisted the top off his water and drank it in one long swallow. Tossing it into the recycling bin, he ordered another. Children gathered around a red makeshift pond with hundreds of yellow rubber duckies floating in it. They held little blue-and-white lifesaver rings in their tiny hands, tossing them in an attempt to land them around the ducks' necks. Surprisingly, a few had actually scored high enough to win a small stuffed animal. He wondered if Gunner had stood on that very spot, playing the same game. He'd called Alice on the way to the fairgrounds to see if she'd still be there when he arrived. They'd missed each other by an hour, but she'd reassured him that she'd bring Gunner by over the weekend.

The sun was low in the sky, casting a golden glow over the towering rides. A Ferris wheel carried passengers to the highest point at the fairgrounds while a human slingshot launched its tethered passengers into the air. Terrorizing screams mixed with laughter. The salty scent of dry roasted peanuts danced among those of fried mozzarella sticks and funnel cake.

He made his way down the wide aisles, still unable to find a place to sit. He'd opted out of bringing one of the walkers with a built-in seat, thinking he'd have the stamina to make it around the fairgrounds. He'd overestimated his abilities and regretted his ambitious decision. His ten thousand steps a day on the ranch were evenly spaced between sunrise and sunset. Right now, his body ached as if he had walked ten thousand steps in the last hour.

"I'll never find her in all these people," Brady said aloud. He thought about sitting on the ground, then feared he wouldn't be able to get up again. "Don't they have seats at these things?" There had to be other disabled people there.

He'd seen a handful of people roll past in wheelchairs, but he'd been the only person using a walker. Of course he was. Most people knew their own limitations. He had to push his limits daily. After the multiple sessions he'd had today both in hippotherapy and with Shane at the rodeo school, he was in no condition to walk around the county fairgrounds. "What the hell was I thinking? Sheila wouldn't even want to be seen with me like this."

"Brady?" He turned to see Thomas holding a gigantic soda and a salted pretzel. What was with the guy and pretzels?

"Hey, man. How are you doing?" Brady tried to keep it casual. His legs began to shake. "Please help me. I need to sit down."

Thomas sat his soda on the ground and ducked behind a vendor's stand, returning with a folding chair. He flipped it open and placed it behind Brady. "What are you doing here? Sheila and I were just talking about planning an outing tomorrow or the next night and bringing everyone from Dance of Hope here."

Brady hadn't been happier to sit in all his life. "You were?"

"It was Sheila's idea, but Gracie and I agreed to come along and help out. So did Sheila. We plan to talk to everybody about it in the morning."

Brady laughed. He would have come to the county fair with Sheila tomorrow, probably dropped off at the entrance, using the proper walker, and he wouldn't be all hot, sweaty and disgusting. "That's wonderful."

"Why are you using this walker? It's not meant for this." Thomas waved his hands in the air for emphasis. "Never mind. I know exactly what this is about. Let me get Sheila."

"Wait." If Thomas suspected his feelings for Sheila then there was a good chance Gracie did too. He didn't want to risk Sheila's job. "This was a bad idea. A really bad idea."

Thomas squatted in front of him. "I think it was a sweet romantic gesture that she'll definitely appreciate. And a really bad idea."

"I don't want her to get in trouble."

"If you ever repeat this to anyone, I will deny it. My wife does not have to know you're here. Give me a few minutes, and I'll take care of it." He reached for his soda and took a bite of his pretzel. "Just sit tight."

Before Brady had a chance to argue, Thomas disappeared into the throng of fairgoers. Brady looked around at the able-bodied men walking with their arms around their girlfriends. They had it so easy and they didn't even realize it. Every step he ever took he'd taken for granted. He glanced down at his jeans and navy blue T-shirt. He didn't have much of a selection at Dance of Hope. What he had served dual-purpose—both therapy and leisure. At least they had on-site laundry.

He stretched out his legs, allowing himself to lean back against the metal chair. It wasn't perfect, but it did quite nicely. He wished he could tuck his bright silver walker away somewhere.

"I can't believe my eyes." Sheila's hand flew to her chest. "I thought Thomas was kidding when he said you were here. Brady, what are you— How did you—"

"Because I wanted to see you, and I hitched a ride." There he'd said it. It was out in the open. No hiding. No denying it. "Tell me it was worth it."

Brady tucked his legs and stood. Sheila grabbed his elbow to support him. "I can't believe you did this for me."

"I wanted to feel normal for a night. I don't know what I expected. I knew you were with Gracie and Thomas and it's not like we can walk around in public holding hands, I just wanted to see you somewhere other than Dance of Hope or the hospital."

Sheila wiped her eyes with the back of her hand. "You're making me cry, Brady Sawyer—and nobody makes me cry."

"Aw, sugar, don't shed a tear on my account." Brady smiled down on her. "I should go and let you be with your friends. I'm sure there are other people here who know you and you shouldn't be seen with me."

"I can't let you leave. Then what would have been the point of your coming?" Her voice was soft and soothing. For a moment he thought she'd reach up and kiss him. If only she had. "I'd fail as your doctor if I just left you here. There are some bleachers two rows over—can you make it that far?"

"I've had a little rest. I'll be okay to walk over there. It was the walk across the parking lot that did me in." The setting sun warmed the color of her skin. She appeared almost ethereal before him in a pair of khaki shorts and a thin ivory chemise. "You are so beautiful."

"I think you're going to be the death of both of us."

He already felt like he was in heaven when she was near.

Chapter Nine

"How are you feeling?" Sheila still couldn't believe Brady had walked all the way from the main road to the fairgrounds just so he could see her.

"Renewed." Brady checked his watch. "It's almost ten thirty. I guess we should call it a night."

They'd been sitting on the bleachers talking for the past couple of hours. Sheila figured if anyone from the hospital spotted them together, it would appear platonic enough. She'd heard every story from his youth ranging from him falling out of a pecan tree in his parents' backyard to competing in his first rodeo event. She'd shared a few stories of her own, but mostly she enjoyed listening to him. His rural Texas life had been much more exciting than her Colorado Rockies suburbia.

"I have the next two days off from work," Sheila said. "Unless you're in a hurry to head home."

"Home." Brady sighed. "I haven't seen home in three and a half months, almost to the day." He faced her. "How would you like to do me a humongous favor?"

"That all depends." Sheila felt anticipation begin to grow in her stomach. "What's the favor?"

"Take me home."

"Brady, I don't—"

"Please. Cherry Spring's about fifteen minutes from here. I've asked my dad, I've asked Alice, and nobody will take me home. I just want to see and feel my things. I promise I'll go straight back to Dance of Hope afterward."

Sheila didn't see the harm in driving him to his house for a few minutes. She couldn't understand why no one had done it sooner and wondered if there was something there he wasn't supposed to see. She wished she had Alice's or his father's phone number to double-check with them before venturing out there, but those numbers were on file at the hospital. He was a grown man. He could face whatever was waiting for him, if there was anything to see.

"On one condition," Sheila warned. "You're going to wait by the entrance while I pick up the car."

"That wouldn't be very gentlemanly of me. I insist on walking with you. It's late, it's dark. If you don't want to take me home because of that, so be it. I'll take tomorrow off from physical therapy and take a cab. Hell, I'll ride a horse if I have to."

Sheila rolled her eyes. There was no stopping him when he set his mind to something. "Okay, you win." Sheila stood. "Let's go."

"Will you do me another favor?"

Sheila put her hands on her hips. "What now?"

Brady laughed. "You're so cute when you're frustrated. I could just kiss you."

She held up her hands and backed away. "No kissing. If we go back to your place, there will be no kissing."

A couple next to them started giggling.

"Do you see what she's like?" Brady said to the couple. "I can't get any lovin'."

Sheila swatted him. "You are such a liar."

Brady grabbed her wrist and pulled her toward him, their lips inches apart. "I'll behave if you behave," Brady whispered as he released her.

"What's your other favor, Mr. Sawyer?" She asked warily.

"Ride the carousel with me." Brady began to walk toward it, not bothering to wait for her to respond. "I have my reasons," he called over his shoulder. "I'll tell you when we're actually on it."

Curiosity got the best of her, and within minutes, she found herself bobbing up and down on a painted carousel horse.

She held her hands out wide. "I haven't ridden one of these since I was a little girl." She looked over at Brady watching her with a big grin plastered across his face. "Okay, tell me why this was so important to you."

"When I was a kid, this was the one ride my mom would get on. She and I rode the carousel dozens of times whenever we went to a carnival or a county fair. It was our thing. She loved it. And I miss it—I miss her." Brady turned away from her. "I just wanted a little piece of my old life tonight."

Sheila wanted to comfort him, but she wasn't sure if that's what he wanted. She hadn't lost a parent or experienced half the things he had in his life. Throwing caution to the wind, she reached out for him, not caring who saw them. Sometimes you just had to give somebody a shoulder to lean on. Brady started to take her hand when the carousel slowed to a stop. Their ride was over.

They made their way across the parking lot together in the dark. Brady refused to allow her to walk alone and she respected him for that. It meant a lot to him and she reasoned he'd had quite a few things taken away from him over the past three and a half months.

They rode in the silence of the car. Part of her wanted him to take her hand just as he'd done on the Fourth of July, but he kept to himself. That was good. At least one of them had some common sense. Her judgment was clearly off tonight. First hanging out with him at the fair, followed by a carousel ride and now driving him home. Each hour took her further down a road she shouldn't travel. Such as the long dirt drive to his house. She didn't know what to expect next.

Brady leaned forward, almost on the edge of his seat, trying to see in the moonlight. She flicked on her high beams so they could both get a better view of his house and property. It was a small ranch, she guessed a handful of acres, but neat. The front yard was all grass and recently mowed. From what she could see of the pastures, they didn't seem too overgrown. Nothing some grazing horses wouldn't fix. Not that she knew a lot about grazing horses.

She parked the car and turned off the engine. "Brady, is everything as you remember it? Has something changed?"

Brady opened the car door and removed his walker

from the backseat. "My house never looked this good before. That railing over there was broken." He pointed to the front stairs. "And the shutter on that window above the door was hanging loose." He walked closer to the house and ran his hand over the clapboard siding. "I don't believe it."

"What? Brady, what's going on?"

"My dad fixed up my house and painted it. I'd been saving my money for months and my dad did it for me."

"Wow! That was nice of him." Brady glared at her. "That wasn't nice of him?" Sheila didn't understand.

Brady shook his head. "It was very generous of him, but I know my dad can't afford it, and—" Brady removed his hat and raked his hand through his hair. "You're going to think I'm the most ungrateful man on the face of the earth, but it meant so much to me to buy this house and be the one to fix it up. My dad has always done things for me. This was my project. He knew that."

"I'm sure he meant well, Brady." Sheila turned off the headlights and joined him near the porch. "Your dad's a good man." She wasn't sure what John's motivation had been, but she could see the situation from both men's point of view.

"Yes he is, but it's more than that, Sheila." Brady rubbed his eyes. "My dad did this because he didn't think I'd ever be able to do it myself. That's why he and Alice didn't want me to see my house all this time. Then I would have known they didn't have faith in my recovery. I thought they believed in me." Brady reached under the front porch step and removed a hidden key. "I'm almost afraid to see what they did inside."

So was she. She prayed they hadn't gone through his house and made it wheelchair accessible. She'd heard of families doing that to patients without their permission and it wasn't always welcomed. Having a physical disability didn't mean a person couldn't think for themselves any longer. Especially someone in Brady's condition. Even at this point in his recovery, he'd most likely be able to get around his entire house on his own.

Sheila placed her hand on his back as he unlocked the door. It opened silently and Brady mumbled something under his breath. "They lubricated my front door. I liked it squeaky. It gave it character."

He flipped the light switch on the wall and surveyed the living room. It was pretty sparse and Sheila feared John and Alice had removed much of his furniture. She chewed on her bottom lip, uncertain how he'd react.

"At least they didn't touch anything in here." He trudged around the room.

"Oh! It's supposed to look like this?" Sheila quickly covered her mouth. "I'm sorry. I wasn't disparaging it."

"Yes, you were. It's okay. I'm a guy. This is what my house looks like." Brady strode into the kitchen and turned on the lights. He returned satisfied. "I did have a few scatter rugs down that I don't see, but I can live with that. Right now that's probably for the best, especially with this clumsy thing." Brady gestured to the walker.

"Actually, I believe I have a cane in my trunk." Sheila backed to the door. "Let me check. Be right back."

Sheila needed a minute to gather her thoughts. The intimacy of being inside Brady's home had caught her off guard. Visiting someone's house was such a casual and normal thing to do, yet with Brady if felt like the beginning of something much bigger. And she wasn't so sure she minded that idea. She should mind. She should wait for him out on the front porch and take him straight back to Dance of Hope. But that wasn't what she wanted. She wanted to tempt fate. She wanted to see where tonight would lead, knowing full well whatever happened would have to end here. She could allow herself one evening alone with him, if only to get Brady Sawyer out of her system.

She grabbed the cane from her car and bounded up the porch stairs, reining herself in just before she opened the screen door. "Here." She breathlessly thrust the cane at him.

Brady laughed. "Sweetheart, I desperately need a shower after my fairgrounds walkathon. Would you be terribly offended if I took one?"

"No, go right ahead." Sheila looked around. "Do you mind if I use your bathroom?"

"Sure, it's upstairs. I'll show you."

Sheila was impressed with his ability to climb the narrow stairs to the second floor using only the banister for support. She'd always wondered how people got furniture upstairs in the olden days. The stairways didn't seem wide enough. She excused herself to the bathroom, returning minutes later to find Brady standing in the doorway of a room down the hall. She padded its length, peeking under his arm. He stepped aside so she could see into the room.

"Gunner's?" It was decorated in red, white and blue, Texas flags and bull rider decals adorned every wall. It needed a good going-over. A child's room should never be vacant for so long that it got dusty or grew cobwebs. She had a suspicion Brady was thinking the same thing.

He held her face in his hands and tilted it up to him. "Thank you for bringing me here. This means the world to me."

Instead of kissing her on the mouth as she'd expected—wanted—he kissed her on the top of the head and then released her. Well, she'd asked him not to kiss her and he kept it platonic. Too platonic.

Sheila started to head downstairs, then thought better of it. She didn't want to be too far away in case he needed her. Now she felt like his father and Alice. He was capable of taking a shower by himself without her hovering. She still couldn't bring herself to go down the stairs. Instead, she peeked into the other two bedrooms. One was completely empty. The other she assumed was his. A double bed and a dresser, sparsely decorated with the exception of trophies and champion belt buckles.

She picked up one of them, the metal cold and surprisingly heavy in her hand. She'd seen them on television and on people when she was out, but she'd never touched one before. There was something personal and intimate about handling Brady's buckle. Too intimate. She placed it back on the dresser. She shouldn't be snooping around his room. She turned off the light and stepped into the hallway just as he opened the bathroom door wearing nothing but a towel.

"Oh my." Sheila's eyes traveled exactly *there*. The one spot they shouldn't have landed.

Brady tilted his head, trying to make eye contact. "Is there something I can help you with?"

Sheila knew her cheeks were flaming red and there was no hiding it. She met his gaze and smiled. "I'm going to go downstairs."

Sheila couldn't get downstairs fast enough. She ran over to the couch, buried her face in the pillow and screamed. She'd never wanted a man more in her entire life.

BRADY ENJOYED THE effect he'd just had on Sheila. At least he knew he still had *it*, scars and all. Maybe they'd work in his favor. Women always went crazy for pirates and war heroes. Many of them had scars. Maybe there was something to it.

He pulled on a fresh pair of jeans and a clean T-shirt and joined her in the living room. Going down the stairs definitely wasn't as easy as going up them. Going up he could pull himself along, going down he had the sensation he was about to land on his face at any moment.

Sheila had managed to find two Cokes in the refrigerator and an unopened bag of chips in the pantry. "I made us a little party, hope you don't mind."

"I don't mind at all. Make yourself at home." Brady took in the sight of Sheila in his living room. She fit. She seemed at ease kicked back on his couch with her soda and chips. The only other woman who'd ever been in his house was Alice and she had always appeared very awkward. Which was surprising considering they'd grown up together and had practically lived at each other's houses most of their lives. But she'd always seemed tense here. Even before he made an offer, he'd brought her to get her opinion. Although she'd said that she liked the house, it wasn't to her taste.

"I couldn't really see outside, but it looks like you have stables back there."

"Come on." Brady motioned to her. "I'll give you a tour."

Sheila set her Coke on a makeshift coaster. "I don't think we should. You've put your body through enough tonight."

"We're not going to walk, we're going to ride." He enjoyed her wide-eyed expression. "Will you trust me?" He held out his hand to her.

"I'll trust you up until the point I don't trust you."

Brady led her through the mudroom, and flicked on the outdoor lights. Once outside, he removed the cover from a yellow-and-black four-wheeler. He climbed on top, turned the key and checked to make sure it still ran. Satisfied, he cut the engine and waved her over.

"Are you sure this is safe?" She stood beside him, staring at the seat.

"Are you a four-wheeler virgin?" Brady asked. "I promise to be gentle. We won't go more than ten miles an hour." He scooted forward and patted the seat behind him. "Now hop on and wrap your arms around my waist."

She did as he instructed and he immediately regretted it. The feel of her breasts pressed against his back brought all his body parts to life, one in particular. *Think football. Think bulls and bucking broncs. Think poker.* Brady attempted to distract himself, praying her hands didn't accidentally shift any lower.

He started the engine and pulled around to the front of his house.

"This small round enclosure is actually a training pen for horses. I had hoped to one day breed and train some of my own, but that's a long way off. The previous owner had a nice little training business here."

He continued past the first pasture and down to the stables.

"How many horses do you have?" She asked over his shoulder, her cheek pressed close against his ear.

"Two." His father had moved them to his property after Brady's accident. "I'll have to remove all these old hay bales and the grain I had stored from the spring before they can come home. I'll need new bedding too. This whole stable needs to be thoroughly checked for snakes and critters. Three and a half months is a long time to sit empty."

Sheila tightened her grip around his waist and rested her head against his shoulder. The gesture warmed him in ways it shouldn't. When she'd first climbed on behind him, he'd thought his feelings were pure lust. With each stop on their ranch mini tour, he noticed her clinging to him tighter and it felt good. It felt like home.

"And lastly." He pulled alongside a chicken coop that had definitely seen better days. "This is for the chickens I don't have. Gunner wants pygmy goats, so I'll probably just tear the coop down and build some form of an enclosure for the goats instead."

He parked the four-wheeler next to the back stairs.

When Sheila climbed off, he immediately missed her touch. She waited for him to join her, offering her shoulder for support since he'd left his cane inside the back door. He wrapped his arm around her, flashing back to the men he'd seen at the county fair walking with their wives and girlfriends. Sheila fit nicely under his arm. The same way she fit nicely in his house. If he was a sentimental guy, he'd say she was made for him. He wasn't sentimental, though. Not in the least. But he still believed she was made for him.

"I don't know what this thing is between you and me, but I'd like to ask you for another favor." Brady popped a DVD into the player and joined her on the couch, clicking on the television with the remote. "I've seen you do your job and I appreciate how much it means to you. I want to share mine with you, at least what I can share of it from here."

Brady heard Sheila swallow hard. Even in the dimly lit room, he noticed her fingers dig into her thighs. Her trepidation took him a little by surprise. He already knew she was against him competing again, but he didn't understand why she would be opposed to seeing some of his past performances. Clearly, he had survived them and it wasn't like they were watching footage from his final ride atop GhostMaker. Or had she already seen it?

"Have you seen me ride before?"

Sheila shook her head. "No."

"Do you know anything about it or want me to explain—"

"I'm aware of how it works." Her features remained expressionless. "At least I have a general idea."

He wished she would ask him a question or two about riding or express some interest in an important part of his life. "Okay, what aren't you telling me?"

"Truth?"

"Please." The DVD stopped spinning in the player and the room fell uneasily silent.

"I'm okay with the rodeo and all the other events. At least I think I am. But they weren't what landed you in my OR. It's you talking about getting back on a bull that gets to me. There are multiple events you can compete in. Why bull riding?"

"I believe in facing my fears head-on."

Sheila's brows rose at his confession.

"Yes, a part of me is scared to get back on a bull," he said. "But a bigger part is scared not to."

"And I'm afraid we'll watch this video and it will give you even more incentive to ride again. It terrifies me. I'm not just saying that from a doctor's perspective. I— Whatever this is—I don't want to think about you putting yourself in a position to get hurt again. The night you were admitted did something to me. *You* do something to me." Sheila sighed. "I will watch this because I know how much it means to you. So if you're going to play it, do it now before I change my mind."

Brady hadn't time to process her admission before she grabbed the remote from him and pressed Play. "This is—um—a highlight reel from last year that one of my sponsors compiled." He shifted slightly so he could watch the screen and her at the same time. She sucked in a breath the instant the chute gate swung wide. Brady had been so concerned with her reactions he hadn't factored in his own.

The first highlight was a bull ride from the San Antonio Stock Show & Rodeo atop Land Mine. As the bull bucked and twisted, his adrenaline rose. Instinctively he turned his palm up as if he had a bull rope in hand. He tightened his grip and closed his eyes as the next one played from the La Fiesta de los Vaqueros Tucson Rodeo in Arizona when he successfully rode Cajun Fury. It had been one of his most perfect eight-second rides even though the bull had surprised him and spun away from his hand. He could still feel the muscular animal breathing between his thighs before the chute opened. The smell of the rosin, the taste of the arena dirt and the clang of the bull rope's metal bell. He inhaled deeply as if he were actually in the arena taking it all in.

Then he remembered where he was. His eyes shot open. He was almost afraid to look at Sheila. He braved a quick glance as a highlight from Casper, Wyoming, played. She sat perched on the edge of the couch, smiling at him. She turned back to the screen and continued to watch each event until the reel ended.

Sheila clicked off the television and scooted back against the couch. "Okay, so maybe I don't understand how it all works," she finally said. "But I get where you're coming from. I respect your wanting to honor your mom and I can even appreciate your drive to compete. While you didn't always land on your feet during those however many events, you did walk away relatively unscathed. That still doesn't mean I like it."

Brady had expected questions, concerns, or possibly an argument. He definitely hadn't anticipated her understanding his passion. At least not without a lot of convincing. That was good wasn't it? Then why was he more nervous than he'd been before he played the DVD?

"Would you consider watching me compete someday?" he asked.

She laughed nervously. "You need to ask me that question again at a later date."

A later date was her polite way of saying *if you ever compete again.* He could live with that. It wasn't a no. It was a start. "I know Dance of Hope is for my own good, but do you have any idea when I might be able to come home?"

"Brady, you can go home anytime you want, although I strongly advise you to wait a bit longer since you live alone. You don't need me or Dance of Hope to release you." Sheila slipped off her shoes and tucked a long bare leg beneath her. "The only thing you need me to do is sign off on your driving because Dr. Mangone hadn't cleared you for that. You'll need to be off all the heavy-duty pain killers and able to adequately brake and accelerate for me to give you the go-ahead. There's a test they conduct at Dance of Hope that you can take whenever you want. You'll have to pass it a few consecutive times and then you can drive again."

"I haven't taken any painkillers since my first week at Dance of Hope. You can even check my prescription bottles at the cottage."

"That's great. I had no idea."

"You didn't ask. The nurses and Marissa did, but

you've been too busy avoiding me." Brady instantly felt guilty for bringing up their rift. He was the one who'd asked her to leave and then yelled at her for trying to help him. He'd been an ass and she was right to avoid him.

"And they should ask. It's their job to monitor your meds. For the record, I was not avoiding you. Okay, today I was. But only because of how we left things last week."

"You mean after I kissed you."

"Do you really want to rehash this right now?" Sheila asked.

"No, but I would like to kiss you again, if you'd let me." Brady knew he shouldn't push, but he'd hate himself in the morning if he didn't at least try.

"I thought we discussed this at the fairgrounds." Sheila's smile led him to believe she might say yes.

"You discussed it, I argued."

"True. You did argue." She pressed her lips together slightly as if she were blotting lipstick on a tissue.

"Spend the night with me." It wasn't a question—it was a statement. Desire had grown to need and he was tired of tiptoeing around it.

"That's way more than kissing." She looked down at her hands. "Is that what you had in mind when you brought me here?"

"You were in the driver's seat so you brought me here. And no, I didn't have that in mind. I still don't have *that* in mind. It may have crossed it, but that's not why I'm asking you to stay. Tonight has been a roller coaster. I wanted to feel normal so I decided to meet you at the county fair only to realize I wasn't prepared enough to handle it on my own. I watched all these couples going by and realized how much I want that. And I'll admit, I want that with you. I understand and respect why we can't be together, but—"

"But what?" Sheila moved closer to him on the couch.

He reached out and tucked a strand of hair behind her ear. "When I'm with you, I feel like I can do anything. You make me feel whole again. I haven't felt whole since long before the accident. There was always something missing and I can't help but wonder if that something was you. You fill this big void in my life and I keep telling myself it's wrong. And I know you're doing the same thing. But is it? Is it really wrong to want you as much as I do—to feel the way I feel about you?

"Brady, true feelings are never wrong. Sometimes we have to rein in our hearts, but a very wise woman told me recently we can't help who we fall in love with. And I'm not saying you've fallen in love with me or that I've fallen in love with you, but I find it impossible to deny that I have a real attraction to you. One I can't escape."

Brady cupped the back of her head and drew her closer to him. "Tell me I can kiss you."

Sheila's eyes fluttered closed. "You can kiss me." Her voice was barely a whisper.

His mouth slanted over hers, her lips soft and gentle against his. She eased her body into his arms, splaying her fingertips across his chest. Her arms wound around his neck, guiding him closer. "Tell me you'll spend the night."

Sheila nodded slowly. Tilting her head back exposing her neck and throat, he nudged her thin cotton chemise lower, exposing the white lace of her bra. One peaked nipple strained against the material, begging to be freed.

"I need to hear you say the words," Brady whispered against her breast.

"I'll stay the night with you," Sheila moaned. She released herself from his embrace, long enough to raise her arms, allowing him to lift her shirt over her head. She reached behind her back, and unfastened her bra, exposing her breasts to him. "But only tonight."

"You're exquisite." Brady dipped his head to taste one hardened nipple and then the other. Rolling his thumbs over them, he trailed kisses across her chest and up her neck until he reached her mouth again. He stood, holding his hand out to her. "Let me make love to you in my bed."

She allowed him to lead the way upstairs, his body aching in anticipation. Brady had intended to take the lead in the bedroom too, but Sheila had other plans.

She guided him to the bed and patted the edge for him to sit. Wearing only a pair khaki shorts, she stood between his thighs, allowing him to unfasten them and ease the zipper down. Before he could release her from their confines, she stepped back and slowly slid them past her hips until she stood before him wearing only a pair of red lacy underwear. He hadn't expected her to wear something so tantalizing. Then again, he was learning to expect the unexpected when it came to Sheila.

"It's your turn, cowboy." She closed the distance

between them, allowing him to take one of her breasts into his mouth again as she urged his shirt up and over his shoulders. "Tonight I want to explore all of you."

Brady inhaled sharply. She had seen his scars before. She'd even touched them during his exams, but this was different. She eased him backward on the bed and he wanted nothing more than to pull her down on top of him to hide his scarred body and lose himself in her. She resisted. Unfastening his jeans, he lifted his hips, allowing her to free him fully. Lying there exposed to her, there was no denying his attraction. There was no hiding from her penetrating gaze either.

Any fears he had of her rejecting his body faded when she climbed onto the bed beside him. Trailing her fingers along every scar, she followed them with featherlight kisses. It was as if time stood still. Brady's breathing slowed in rhythmic pace with hers as she explored his body one inch at a time. He'd never experienced such tenderness—such passion and joy—at the same time. And when she finally straddled him, joining their bodies together, she completed him.

Sheila was his, if only for one night. At least he'd know what it felt like to love her.

Chapter Ten

Sheila awoke the next morning, deliciously sore. Nestled against his chest, she peeked under the sheets. Yep, he was still there—all of him. It had never felt so good to be so bad. She didn't know if sex with Brady always felt that incredible or if it was because she wasn't supposed to be having sex with Brady. Either way, it had been more romantic and amazing than she had imagined.

Sheila ran her hand up his chest, his scars brutal reminders of his career choice. Forbidden romance or not, it didn't change his plan to risk everything atop a one-ton animal again. After watching the DVD, she could better understand his passion for bull riding, but she still didn't think she could live with it.

Sun filtered through the windows, bathing them in renewed hopes and dreams. She'd grown up believing every day was a fresh start regardless of the prior days' events. Sheila didn't know if she should consider last night a mistake or the chance at a future together. She wanted Brady to have a future filled with options. Once she spoke with Kay Langtry about the possibility of his working at Dance of Hope, maybe he'd realize the world wasn't as black-and-white as he thought it was.

Brady stirred beside her. She rubbed her bare leg against his thigh while she began kissing his chest, working her way down. She wanted to wake Brady in the best way possible. His fingers entwined with hers, pulling her up to his mouth. He shifted his weight beneath her until she was sitting astride him.

"If you're going to wake me up," Brady growled, "this is how we're going to start the morning."

By the time she made it out of bed two hours later, her legs shook with pleasure. The man was insatiable and that suited her just fine. It had been years since Sheila had felt this free. She heard a light knock at the bathroom door. She opened it, wearing nothing but a smile. Brady gave her an appreciative glance before making his way to the sink. Before she'd made it back to the bedroom, she felt a hand around her waist pulling her toward him.

"Brady, we have to stop." She half crawled, half walked into his bedroom and collapsed across the bed. "I am forbidding you from physical therapy today." Sheila noticed the time on the bedside table. It was almost eleven o'clock. "You need to let someone at Dance of Hope know that you're home and not lying unconscious inside your cottage. They're probably wondering where you are."

"I texted Thomas this morning when you were still sleeping." Brady eased into bed beside her. "He said he'd tell everyone I'd be missing therapy today and that I should say hello to you."

Sheila sat upright. "He said what?"

Brady laughed. "I'm just kidding." He attempted to tug her into his arms, but she escaped his grasp. "You don't think I would honestly betray you like that, do you?"

"I hope not." Sheila began to relax again. "I need to take a shower. Alone."

Brady pouted. "Solo showers are no fun."

"That's a good thing, because I've had all the fun I can handle this morning."

"Party pooper." Brady stood. The scar from where the bull had punctured his lung mocked her from across the room. She quickly ducked into the bathroom and closed the door, willing the image of his lifeless body out of her head. "Sheila? Are you all right?"

She pulled back the shower curtain surrounding the claw-foot tub and turned the knobs. "I'm wonderful." Sheila's voice cracked. "I just remembered I had promised Thomas and Gracie I'd help them take everyone to the county fair this afternoon." It wasn't an outright lie. She had remembered, just not at that precise moment. "You're welcome to join us."

Sheila climbed into the tub, drawing the shower curtain around her. The warm water washed away Brady's kisses—his touch—bringing her back to reality. She was his doctor, and the second she walked out his front door, she needed to maintain that image and that image alone.

She emerged from the bathroom, wrapped in one of his towels. When she didn't see him in the bedroom, she assumed he'd gone downstairs. She put on yesterday's clothes, once she found them, trying to figure out how she would drop Brady off at Dance of Hope in the middle of the day without detection. It was impossible. She certainly couldn't chance running into Gracie or Thomas wearing the same thing she'd worn the night before. They needed to stop by her house on the way home so she could change. Then if anyone questioned them, she could just say she'd driven Brady to the hospital for an appointment.

She sat on the edge of the bed, her head in her hands.

"Hey, what is it?" Brady said from the doorway, leaning against it for support.

"I was just thinking up a lie we could tell everyone in case we get caught when I drop you back off at the ranch. But first, we need to stop by my house so I can change. I'm already exhausted trying to cover us up."

"So it's not my imagination, there is an us," Brady said.

Sheila stared at him. "I only meant for this to be one night. I know I'm not exactly old-fashioned, but I think having sex with somebody multiple times within a twelve-hour period constitutes there being an us. I just haven't figured out how us works or fits into our lives." She left out the part where giving her heart to a stubborn bull rider terrified her more than anything else. "Where were you just now?"

"Gunner's room." With the aid of his cane, Brady made his way to the dresser and grabbed a clean set of clothes. "I couldn't stand the thought of three inches of dust all over his things any longer. I can't wait to tell him on Saturday that I'll be coming home soon.

Listen, I appreciate your offer to join all of you at the county fair today, but I'm going to pass. There's a lot I want to do around here, so you don't have to worry about coming up with a lie. You don't have to drive me back to Dance of Hope. I'll have my dad do it when he gets off work today."

Sheila shook her head. "Brady, I can't in good conscience leave you here alone, and I've already committed to another obligation today."

Brady laughed. "That's okay, I'm not asking you to stay. I realize you have things to do. So do I."

Sheila tried to come up with a tactful way to explain things. "You're staying at Dance of Hope, free of charge I might add, because you weren't ready to live here by yourself. You can't stay here all day, walk up and down stairs and go about your life and then head back to Dance of Hope and eat their food, use their equipment and sleep in their beds at night. You have to choose one, Brady. Either you live at Dance of Hope or you live here. If you're capable of spending the day alone here, then you need to move on and out of Dance of Hope so that spot is available for somebody else in need."

"You said it was my decision." Brady seemed shocked at what she was telling him.

"It is your decision. But you have to make a decision." Sheila searched the room for her shoes, remembering she'd left them downstairs last night. "I've already advised you to stay at Dance of Hope a while longer. At least until you have some systems in place, like how you'll get to physical therapy every day and how you'll go grocery shopping. You can arrange for a home health aide to stop in a few days a week. You have choices and maybe you should be making these decisions sooner than later. But I'd be remiss as your physician if I didn't make sure you had a plan in place. Splitting your time between Dance of Hope and here is not a plan. Those spaces are too valuable."

"You're asking me to go back with you."

"I'm asking you to make a decision about your future. It's not just about today. You're working so hard to rebuild your body and I know you want to come home, but you have to realize you'll need some help when you do. I'm afraid if I leave you here, you won't want to go back, and I feel you need to allow yourself the time to plan for your immediate future." Sheila hated transitioning back into her role as Brady's doctor, but his well-being was her first priority. "I'll be downstairs while you shower. I have to leave shortly, so if you can let me know sooner rather than later, I'd appreciate it. You've already been at Dance of Hope for a month, what's another week or even a few days?"

"Can't you go home and do what you have to do and then come back?" he asked. "Wherever it is that you live. Shame on me for not asking you before."

"I live ten minutes from the hospital. I don't even know how far we are from Dance of Hope."

"It's about fifty minutes from here," Brady said.

"And I'm another fifteen minutes past Ramblewood." Sheila mentally added up the drive. "That's a two-and-a-half-hour round-trip. Plus there are people waiting for me at Dance of Hope."

Brady turned away from her. "I'll meet you downstairs and we'll leave together."

Sheila breathed a sigh of relief. She respected Brady for wanting to do it on his own, but he wasn't ready yet. And she wasn't sure she was ready for this relationship. The logistics after one night together set her teeth on edge. Relationships shouldn't be hidden or complicated. They should come naturally. As easy as it had been to fall into bed with Brady last night, in the cold light of day, she didn't think they'd survive the obstacles ahead of them.

BRADY HAD GONE from feeling like a man to a child in 2.2 seconds. He didn't need a chaperone in his own home. He wanted the freedom to come and go as he pleased. He showered and shaved with the world's worst disposable razor. When the fog cleared in the bathroom, he caught a glimpse of his naked body in the full-length mirror hanging on the back of the bathroom door. He'd been in such a hurry last night he'd forgotten it was there.

He stared at his reflection. If it hadn't been for his face, he wouldn't have recognized himself. The small mirror at Dance of Hope hadn't afforded him a complete view of his upper body. His arms and shoulders were bigger and bulkier than they'd ever been, which explained why his shirts felt increasingly tighter. His legs were thinner, but had still retained some of their former muscle. His trademark six-pack was covered in scars, as was his back.

He ran his fingertips across the fist-size scar over

his ribs. GhostMaker's horn. A smaller exit scar was located in the same position on his back. The scar on his backside from the skin graft they took to cover his puncture wound was the ugliest of them all. He understood why Dance of Hope didn't have full-length mirrors. If he had seen these scars when he'd first arrived, he probably would have fixated on them. Brady knew they'd heal over time. Just the fact that Sheila had kissed every one of them warmed his heart. She didn't judge him by his appearance. She judged him by his career choice. At least she had up until last night. He was still a long way from competing again. He had to find a way to change her mind between now and then. He didn't want her just to accept his decision. It was important that she support it as she'd supported him through his recovery. She was the one good thing that had come out of his accident. Now that she was in his life, he couldn't imagine living without her.

DURING A QUICK stop at Sheila's house, where she'd given him a three-minute tour, Brady had seen a very feminine side of her. She'd decorated her house with whitewashed furniture and off-white linens. Pastel-colored walls and accent pieces added to the atmosphere of serenity. He'd wanted to see her bedroom, but she refused, ushering him out the door before he had a chance to protest.

They'd arrived at Dance of Hope without incident— Sheila choosing the main entrance while Brady hung around the rodeo school before making his way to his cottage. The room he'd spent the past month in felt foreign to him again. Now that he'd had a taste of home, he couldn't get back there fast enough. He tossed around the idea of going with Sheila and the rest of Dance of Hope to the county fair. A huge part of him wanted to hold on to that memory of just the two of them at the fair. A bigger part wanted to see the little kids' faces light up when they got there.

Sheila rode in a separate transport van with Gracie and Kay. He knew he shouldn't make anything of it, but she'd grown increasingly quiet since they'd left his house. Buyer's remorse. That's what his mother had called someone second-guessing their decision about anything. Sheila had maintained a respectable distance from him during their entire trip, until they'd all piled onto the carousel. She'd purchased so many tickets for everyone they'd probably ridden it ten times in total. Sheila claimed she'd done so because it was the one ride many of the kids could go on, and that was all well and good. But he knew she'd also done it for him.

"I can't remember being this tired since my first year at Grace General," Sheila said as she unloaded a cooler from the back of the transport van. "I've had a great time today, but I'm going to call it a night."

"It's still early." Gracie pointed to her watch. "I thought we could head into town. They have a line dancing competition at Slater's Mill tonight."

Brady thought he detected Sheila's knees begin to buckle at the sheer thought of line dancing. She steadied herself against the van. "Not tonight. Work's been unbelievably crazy and I need to sleep. Sweet delicious sleep."

"Fine." Gracie spun to face Brady. "And don't you think you are stealing my husband tonight either. He's taking me line dancing. He just doesn't know it yet." She waved to Thomas across the parking lot. "Get home safely and I'll talk to you tomorrow." Gracie gave Sheila a hug goodbye.

Brady wanted to too, but he couldn't. All he could manage was a "have a good night." Not exactly the romantic sendoff he'd envisioned. He watched Sheila drive out of the parking lot, realizing he still didn't have her phone number. He couldn't even text her goodbye.

Once everyone had settled in for the night, Brady ventured to the fitness room. As tired as he was, he couldn't sleep. And Sheila was right, he needed to make some decisions about his immediate future. He'd waited for this moment for so long, he didn't know what to do with it now that it was here.

After a thirty-minute Nautilus workout, his body had reached its limits for the day. He made his way steadily down the path to the community lounge with the aid of a cane. He could have opted to wheel himself instead of walking, but he refused to make things easier. He was surprised to see Kay Langtry there at such a late hour.

"You couldn't sleep either?" she asked. "All I could think of was the cold fried chicken I knew we had in the refrigerator here and I had to have some. Join me. There's plenty."

Brady laughed when he realized Kay was dressed in her robe and slippers. Her house sat on the opposite end of the parking lot, but still—the woman had traversed the length of a football field in the middle of the night for cold fried chicken.

"You're my kind of woman." Brady helped himself to a piece.

"Let me ask you something." Kay wiped her mouth with a napkin. "Have you thought any more about what you're going to do when you leave here? I don't mean the bull riding—I'm talking about your immediate future."

Brady had been so fixated on getting into shape to compete again, he hadn't given it much thought. "Not yet. I know I need to because I think my time here is coming to an end."

He confided in Kay about visiting his ranch, leaving out certain details. She didn't ask how he'd gotten there and back and he didn't offer either. She explained the aftercare services Dance of Hope offered and advised him to speak with the social worker he'd met with in the hospital to discuss his available assistance options further.

"I know some people opt to rely solely on their disability benefit to support themselves, but I assure you, it won't provide everything you need. I'd like to make you an offer that may be very beneficial to the both of us."

Brady leaned forward in his chair. "You already have me intrigued."

"I'd like you to work here. I could really use someone to help acclimate new residents, talk with parents and loved ones about their concerns and help develop a stronger support system for the people who don't have family here to encourage them. I realize it wouldn't be forever, but between now and when you start competing again, I think we can accomplish a lot together. If it works out, maybe you'd consider staying on when you're not riding. Would you be interested?"

"Yes, very. I don't exactly know how it would work, though. I live almost an hour from here and I can't drive yet."

"We'll have to work those details out. And maybe you'll only be able to work a couple days a week. But as an employee here, you will continue to get free meals and access to all our fitness equipment and of course hippotherapy if you still need it."

Brady had a job offer. A part-time job offer, but a legitimate one...with perks. Too bad he didn't live with Sheila, her house was much closer than his. He mentally kicked himself. The woman wouldn't let him see her bedroom, let alone move in with him. The idea was crazy, but it was a fun thought.

"Thank you, Kay. You have no idea how much I appreciate your faith in me." Brady stood and gave her a hug. "My accident changed my life, but Dance of Hope changed it in a much different way. I would love to give back to the place that helped me live again."

"You're welcome," Kay said. "I should be thanking you. I can't do as much as I would like here and I need to rely on somebody who understands how the process works. You're a perfect fit."

Brady chose to walk back to his cottage after their conversation. It was after midnight and he couldn't help thinking about where he'd been and what he'd been doing twenty-four hours ago. He swiped his key card and opened the door, half hoping he'd find Sheila there. She wasn't. "Why didn't I ask for her phone number?" He had good news to share. It was too late to call his father and calling Alice would wake Gunner. He wondered if Kay had Sheila's number. He debated walking back to the lounge and asking her, then decided against it. Sheila would be asleep anyway and it wasn't worth risking their relationship or her career over. It would keep until he saw her again.

SHEILA HAD CLIMBED into bed four hours ago and she was still tossing and turning, her thoughts rambling. She already missed the feel of Brady's body next to hers. She shouldn't have slept with him last night. And she definitely shouldn't have spent the night. Waking up in somebody's arms meant something. At least it did to her. She ventured to guess if she'd been in his bed tonight, they'd both be fast asleep. Probably exhausted after another marathon sex session. Not that sex was a requirement, but it definitely helped her fall asleep.

She wondered if Kay would take her suggestion to hire Brady seriously. They'd discussed it on the way back from the fairgrounds. Gracie had fully supported the idea and even mentioned that she and Thomas had discussed it a few times. It didn't need to be Dance of Hope, but it needed to be something, anything other than bull riding. Her doubts that he would recover fully had faded. The fear he'd end up back in the hospital had not.

Sitting up, she clicked on the nightstand light. Bed was painfully lonely without Brady. Now that they'd truly crossed an ethical line, she knew she needed to stop being his doctor. It was the right thing to do, and the only way their relationship would work. As much as she kept telling herself they had an impossibly long road ahead of them, her heart wanted to travel that road with Brady.

And the sooner he recovered, the sooner they could have an open relationship. She despised sneaking around. On the flip side, the sooner he recovered, the sooner he would be back on top of a bull. She'd rather sacrifice their relationship than sacrifice his life. There was no hurry to sign off on his recovery and that was what he needed to compete again. Of course, he could get it from another physician if he really wanted to. Her heart would break in two, but she could live without being with Brady. She didn't think she could live in a world without him in it.

Sheila felt herself falling hard for the cowboy. She just hoped it had a soft landing.

Chapter Eleven

Brady hadn't kissed Sheila since they'd spent the night together. Three days had passed and he'd seen her only once. And it had been a very public meeting. He craved the feel of her skin against his, but he'd settle for a platonic conversation. He still hadn't had a chance to tell her about Kay's job offer or get her phone number. It was Saturday and Alice had promised to bring Gunner later that afternoon. He wondered if Sheila would stop in after the hospital. He chastised himself for all his juvenile hoping and wishing. Sheila was working—it was rare when she wasn't. While spending time with her was important, she hadn't seen his son since the Fourth of July and he needed to make sure she understood they were a package deal. He'd dated women in the past who were fine with him having a child as long as Gunner wasn't around. Once Brady returned home, he'd have Gunner 50 percent of the time, so the three of them would be under the same roof at various times. And maybe in time they would add to their family. The thought alone brought a smile to his face. A family with

Sheila sounded perfect, even if he wasn't ready to say the words out loud.

Brady cleared his throat. He was getting way ahead of himself. Before they went any further, he wanted to gauge Gunner's reaction to Sheila. His son had never had false hope of Brady and Alice becoming a couple. He'd been told at an early age that they were friends who'd had a baby together. That was normal for him.

Brady's new normal would change soon. He had an appointment with the social worker on Tuesday morning, which hopefully meant he'd be home before long. He had so much to do between now and then. He hadn't told Alice or his dad about his pending departure from Dance of Hope or that he'd seen the house. His father always stopped by Saturday mornings and he felt he needed to have that conversation face-to-face. He didn't know which made him antsier. Leaving Dance of Hope or their reaction to the news.

Brady laughed. If either of them had stopped by his house over the past few days, they'd probably noticed the unmade bed, and numerous condom wrappers in the bathroom wastebasket. Hey, it was his house. On second thought, his father might assume someone had broken in. Maybe he should have told his dad he'd been home.

Brady was too anxious to sit around. He'd had his first treadmill session that morning and couldn't wait to do it again. He had clocked too much time in the fitness center and had been forced to find an alternative workout method. Eager to get back in competitive form, he walked down to the school's outdoor arena. It was graduation day for the first summer session and they planned to have a full exhibition event. He hoped Alice arrived before it was over. Gunner hadn't been to a rodeo since before the accident. He still gave thanks that his son hadn't been there that day.

Brady had left his walker at the cottage, refusing to use it any longer, even after a strenuous physical therapy session. He was determined to rely solely on his cane. He needed to know he had the strength and stamina to function without relying on a seat being readily available. The ranch had plenty of benches around, they just weren't as convenient as a built-in seat. Not that he would need them.

Being unable to drive and the uneasiness he'd experienced descending the stairs bothered him the most about going home. Abby understood his concerns and had increased his time on the elliptical and stair climber. They'd also been practicing on the stairwell leading to Dance of Hope's loft area. After two rigorous days, he had begun to lose that vertiginous feeling he'd had at home.

Driving had been another story. He'd failed his reflex tests twice. He had more than enough strength to press the gas and brake pedals, but lifting his leg while in a sitting position and moving it back and forth between the pedals needed work. He needed quick reflexes and a full range of motion to compete successfully.

A bull snorted and threw his body against the holding pen, startling Brady. GhostMaker's large head filled his mind, causing him to stumble. He caught himself before he fell. As he turned to look at the bull behind the enclosure, relief overwhelmed him—it looked nothing like the beast that had taken him out. He'd been around hundreds of bulls in his career and had never jumped like that. Nothing like a little posttraumatic stress disorder to get his blood pumping in the morning. Brady made a point to stare the animal in the eyes. He had respect for all of God's creatures, but he needed to get past his anxiety if he ever hoped to compete again.

"I knew I'd find you here." His father gave him a hug hello. "Making friends with the enemy?"

"Something like that." Brady motioned to a picnic table under one of the shade trees. "Why don't we have a seat. I have a few things I need to talk over with you. Starting with the news that I'll probably be going home soon."

"How soon?" his father asked.

"Hopefully within the next week, two at the latest." Brady noticed the vein in his father's forehead begin to pulse. "Have you been to my ranch lately?"

"Not since last weekend." John cleared his throat. "I'll swing by there on the way home today."

"Just a word of warning, I spent the night there on Tuesday, so you might see a few things out of place."

John's eyes grew large. "You did?"

Brady nodded. "I was surprised at how much it had changed since I'd last been home."

"Alice, Gunner and I wanted it to be a surprise."

Brady removed his hat and sat it on the table. "Dad." Brady pressed his palms together in front of his chin. "I have to ask. Did you and Alice fix up the exterior of my house because you thought I wouldn't be able to do it myself?"

John rubbed the back of his neck. "Son, the doctors doubted you'd get this far in your recovery."

"That's not true." Brady shook his head. "Nobody expected me to compete again and they still don't. But Sheila—Dr. Lindstrom—fully expected me to recover to the point where I'd live on my own. Where did all this doubt come from?"

John slammed his hand on the table. "It came from you almost dying. You're a stubborn ass of a man. I should know. I raised you and you're just like me. Only I know when to quit. You won't quit. You've never quit. Your survival rate was next to nothing. You always talk about how blessed you are—well, you are blessed. I'm glad you're blessed because without your mama up in heaven watching over you, you wouldn't be here right now."

"Dad, calm down." Brady couldn't remember ever seeing his father this angry.

"Don't you tell me to calm down." John slammed the table again. "Every night when I go to bed, I pray that you'll come to your good senses and forget this whole bull riding business. I still have nightmares from that day. And yes, we went ahead and fixed up your house. Not because we thought you couldn't, but because we didn't know if we'd have to sell it to cover your long-term expenses. I didn't mean to hurt your feelings. It kept us busy and our minds occupied while you were laying half-dead in the hospital."

Brady sat in shock listening to his father. He didn't know how to react. He was angry, hurt and sympathetic all at the same time.

"I guess you have nothing to say for yourself, huh?"

Brady stared at his father. No. He didn't. "I'm confused, Dad."

"Then get unconfused. You have a child to raise and a family who loves you. Get it together."

"Isn't that what I've been doing? This hasn't been easy. I'm not at a resort, Dad. I bust my butt every day to get stronger."

His father gave him a dismissive wave. "So you can compete again."

"Yes, to compete and to run and play with my son and to take care of myself and to go to work. And for mom."

"Don't you bring your mama into it. She couldn't have handled almost losing you. And you don't even have a job."

"Yeah, Dad, I do." Brady grabbed his hat and stood. "If you hadn't bitten my head off five minutes ago, I would've told you about it."

"So tell me about it now." John rested his arms on the table, casually waiting for Brady to sit back down and tell him about his new job as if their argument hadn't happened.

Brady sighed. The man could turn on a dime. "I was offered a job here, at Dance of Hope."

John's face lit up like Gunner's on Christmas morning as Brady told him about his conversation with Kay. It was only then that Brady realized how worried his father was about him.

SHEILA HAD SPENT most of the night baking cookies. She tried telling herself they were for Dance of Hope and the rodeo school, but they'd started as cookies for Brady and Gunner. She knew Gunner was coming to visit and she wanted to surprise them with a horse-shaped treat. She wanted Brady to know she not only thought about him, she thought of his son too. It was a rarity that she had a Saturday off, especially after having Wednesday and Thursday, but the schedule gods had been on her side this week.

She was nervous about seeing Gunner today. Her relationship with his father had changed and she wasn't sure if he'd pick up on it or not. And since she hadn't told Brady she would be there, she wasn't sure they'd welcome her interrupting their day together. She'd only stay long enough to say hello and give Gunner a cookie. She had never been involved with anyone who had a kid, so she was unfamiliar with the etiquette. She still had to step down as his physician before the relationship developed further. Last night, she'd debated sneaking over to his cottage but had thought the better of it. While she was certain they both would have enjoyed each other's company, it was too high a risk and not one she was willing to take. After she spoke with her attending and Brady was home, then she could steal some private time with him.

Sheila picked up the phone and dialed her mother.

"Hi, honey."

"Hi, Mom, I just wanted to say hello before I ran out for the rest of the day."

"Aren't you working?"

"No, I have the day off."

"Is something wrong? You rarely have Saturdays off."

"No, Mom. Nothing is wrong. I just wanted to call and say hello. You told me I don't call often enough, so I'm calling." Sheila shook her head.

"You should take yourself to one of those spa places today," her mother said. "Treat yourself to a facial and a makeover. You'll feel so much better and then maybe you'll catch yourself a doctor."

"A facial, a makeover and a doctor. That's a tall order." She laughed at her mother's need to micromanage Sheila all the way from Colorado. "I don't need a spa day and I just started seeing someone. I don't know where it will lead, but we'll see."

A *thump* followed by a loud scratching noise blasted through the phone.

"Mom, are you okay?"

"I dropped the phone. Did you say you're seeing someone?"

Wonderful. The news of Sheila having a man in her life was so shocking it caused her mother to drop the phone. That certainly did wonders for her ego.

"Yes, and it's very new. I don't even know if it will last." Sheila heard her mother's hand cover the phone. "Mom, tell Daddy later." She rolled her eyes. She'd told her mom she was seeing someone so she'd stop pressuring her to find a man. Now she was rethinking her decision. It was one thing to bask in morning-after bliss, but considering they hadn't spoken, she didn't know if Brady still felt the same way. They hadn't had an opportunity to discuss it again. In reality, Sheila had no idea where she and Brady stood.

"Tell me all about him. What's his name and where did you meet?"

"We met at the hospital."

"Is he a doctor?"

"He was just visiting." Well he was…for two and a half months. "Listen, Mom, I need to get going. I'm meeting him in a few minutes."

"Why isn't he picking you up? A gentleman picks you up."

Sheila ground her back teeth. She should have known better. Gloating always backfires. "I need to go now. I love you, Mom. Give my best to Dad."

Sheila disconnected the call.

After poring over her closet for an hour, Sheila finally decided on jeans and a white lacy top with strappy sandals. It was casual yet fun and flirty at the same time. She finished bagging her cookies and loaded them into the car. She'd definitely outdone herself this time. They'd still be eating cookies at Christmastime. After she delivered most of them, her nerves began to steadily increase again.

Children were difficult, confusing little people. There was a reason why she didn't have any of her own. Well, there were multiple reasons. One of which was because they scared her. In a hospital setting, Sheila had the upper hand. Out in the wild, she was vulnerable to them.

She spotted Brady with his father and Gunner, playing with a group of other young children. Wonderful.

A herd of them. She stayed far in the background until Brady realized she was standing there and practically ran to see her. Every time she saw him, she noticed marked improvement. She caught herself just as she was about to lean in and kiss him hello. She needed to keep her wits about her.

"This is a surprise," Brady said, and then he leaned closer to whisper, "I would love to kiss you right now."

Sheila wanted to push him away and draw him in at the same time.

"Fireworks Lady!" Gunner came running toward her and crashed into her legs, almost knocking her to the ground. Instead of mutton busting, the kid should try out for peewee football.

"Easy, Gunner. Her name is Dr. Lindstrom." Brady attempted to pry Gunner off her legs.

"I kind of like Fireworks Lady." Sheila squatted down to Gunner's height. "You can call me Doc, Sheila, Linny or whatever you'd like."

"I like Doc," the boy said.

"Daddy likes Doc too." Brady winked.

Sheila shot him a warning look, which made him wink again.

"Hello, Dr. Lindstrom." John Sawyer shook her hand. "It's a pleasure to see you again."

"Please, call me Sheila."

"Or Doc," Gunner added.

"Or Doc." Sheila laughed.

The four of them stood staring at one another. Sheila immediately wondered how much Brady had told his father about their relationship. Based on the looks the two men exchanged, he had divulged more than he should have.

Awkward.

"My son tells me he's going to be working at Dance of Hope soon."

"You are?" Sheila clapped her hands together. "That's wonderful!"

"Pops, I hadn't had a chance to tell her yet." Brady smiled at Sheila. "Kay offered me a job the other day. We just have to work out the logistics of me getting here. It's not exactly next door."

Sheila hadn't thought of that part when she'd suggested Kay hire Brady. "There must be some temporary solution. I'm sure you'll be driving again very soon. If you can accomplish what you have in a little over a month, you can tackle driving. What will you be doing here?"

Sheila was surprised when Brady told her the extent of his job. She'd honestly expected Kay to hire him as a therapist's helper. A job of this magnitude had responsibilities. Even though it was part-time, she couldn't envision Brady walking away from it easily. Sheila smiled. That was why Kay had done it. If she had hired him as a helper, he'd be able to walk away without a second thought. She made a mental note to buy the woman the biggest box of chocolates she could find.

"Are these for us?" Gunner peeked into the tote bag she'd set on the ground by her feet.

"Gunner, it's not polite to go through other people's things." Brady removed Gunner's hands from her bag. "I'm sorry."

"He's right. They are for him." Sheila bent down and pulled a cellophane-wrapped horse cookie out of her bag and handed it to Gunner. "And these are for you two." Sheila handed John and Brady each a cookie. "I have more, but I suspect you don't want me to give him more than one."

"These are adorable." Brady helped Gunner unwrap his cookie. "Did you make these?"

"I did. If I'm not operating on somebody, I'm usually baking."

"Thank you." John gave Sheila a hug. "I'm on my way out, but I'll be back later."

"Alice isn't picking Gunner up?" Brady asked.

"Mommy has a date," Gunner said. "Are you my daddy's date?" he asked Sheila.

"On that note, I'm out of here." John waved goodbye to them.

"Sheila and Daddy are just friends." Brady sat down on the grass beside his son.

"Are you going to have a baby?"

"A baby?" Sheila almost forgot to breathe.

"Mommy and Daddy are friends and they had a baby." Gunner reached up and touched Sheila's belly. "I don't feel a baby. I want a brother or sister."

Brady looked up at Sheila. "One of the problems of being a modern family is explaining to your child that not all friends have babies together."

Sheila felt the color come back into her cheeks. "Whew. I was scared there for a moment. I'm not ready to have kids yet."

"You're not?" Gunner asked, his eyes grew big and sad to the point she thought he might cry.

"I'm not ready to have babies come out of my belly," Sheila corrected. "But I love tickling other people's children." She reached out and playfully grabbed him. "Listen, I don't want to intrude on your father-son time. I just wanted to say hello and bring you a little sweet treat."

"Don't go." Gunner pulled on her hand until she sat down on the grass. "Daddy smiles when you're around. He doesn't smile that big when you're not."

"Is this true?" Sheila asked, knowing full well he wouldn't say no in front of his child.

"It certainly is." Brady ruffled Gunner's hair, lightly brushing her cheek in the process. It had been only a few days and she desperately missed his touch. This felt good. The three of them together on the grass under a shade tree. She could get used to this lifestyle very easily.

Kay walked in their direction. Sheila had let her guard down for a moment too long. She'd make a point to visit with other patients before she left, to eliminate any suspicion.

Gunner yawned. "Daddy. I'm sleepy."

Brady stood, tipping his hat to Kay as she approached. "In a few minutes I'll take you back to the cottage for a quick nap so you'll be awake for the bull riding exhibition. They're already moving the bulls into the holding pens."

Gunner yawned again.

"Brady, do you have a minute?" Kay asked. "There's someone here I would like you to meet."

"Go ahead, I can take him back to the cottage," Sheila said. It would give her a chance to spend a little one-on-one time with Gunner anyway. How else would she know how she felt about a future with Brady if she didn't spend time alone with his son?

Gunner reached up and took Sheila's hand in his. She loved tiny hands. They always felt so soft and smooth. She'd held many of them in the emergency room, but this was different. This was definitely more personal. She wondered if Brady had resembled Gunner at his age.

"Loose bull!" someone shouted.

A woman screamed behind them. Sheila scooped Gunner up into her arms protectively, not knowing where the bull was. They were in an open area between the rodeo school and the hippotherapy center. "I've got you, baby." She started running toward the hippotherapy corral. If she could get them over the fence, they'd be safe.

Gunner started wailing and kicking in her arms. She tightened her grip. The sound of hooves thundered behind them. She couldn't look. She couldn't waste even a fraction of a second to turn around.

Out of nowhere, a piercing whistle sounded repeatedly. The hooves stopped. Sheila reached the fence and pushed Gunner between the bottom and middle rails. "You stay right there. Don't move an inch." Sheila climbed over the fence and dropped down beside him on the other side. She lifted him into her arms again and braved a look behind them.

She heard the earsplitting whistle again.

"Daddy!" Gunner pointed. "That's my daddy."

The bull stood between them and Brady. The animal shook his head from side to side. Pawing at the ground with his massive black hoof. Brady stuck his fingers in his mouth and whistled again and again while waving his hands in the air to attract the bull's attention.

The animal began to charge.

"Brady! No!" Sheila tucked Gunner's head under her chin so he wouldn't see what was about to happen. "Please no—please!" Sheila prayed, tears streamed down her face.

"Daddy!" Gunner cried.

She didn't want to watch, but she found it impossible to turn away. The man she'd fallen in love with— the man she'd helped put back together was about to be trampled by a bull and she was helpless to do anything about it. Within seconds, the animal was upon him and she knew it was the last time she'd see Brady alive.

And then it was over.

Brady grabbed the top fence rail of the rodeo school's round pen and vaulted over it, out of the bull's reach. Another cowboy opened the gate a few feet away and the bull ran through it, into a holding pen.

Sheila fell to her knees, still holding Gunner.

"Sheila." Thomas lifted her up as Gracie removed Gunner from her arms. "I've got you." Thomas turned her toward him. "Are you all right? Does it hurt anywhere?"

Sheila shook her head. She was in shock. She knew she was in shock and she couldn't speak. She reached behind her for Gunner, but Thomas pulled her arms toward him, holding them up in the air to make sure she wasn't injured. "Gracie has Gunner. He's okay. You're okay."

"Brady." His name was barely audible on her lips.

"Brady's okay too," he reassured.

"Let's get them inside" she heard Thomas say to Gracie.

Her head began to swim, the earth seemed to kick out beneath her and then everything went black.

Chapter Twelve

When Sheila awoke, it took her a few moments to realize where she was. Gunner was fast asleep beside her on Brady's bed in the cottage. She sat up and looked around the room. Gracie smiled at her from the bedside chair.

"Look who's awake." She brushed the hair out of Sheila's face. "I've always wondered if you were human—you always appear so invincible. Today you proved you're one of us after all."

"How did I get here?" Various images flashed in her brain. Gunner in her arms. A bull. Brady. "Where's Brady?"

"He was in here a few minutes ago. He just stepped outside."

Sheila swung her legs out of bed and attempted to stand. The room tilted.

"Easy, Sheila. You fainted. Twice."

"Twice?" She tried to shake the cobwebs from her brain. "I've never fainted in my life."

"Surprise." Gracie opened her arms wide. "You did today. And rightfully so. I always knew you were a hero."

"What are you talking about?" Sheila still couldn't process what was going on.

"The way you ran with Gunner in your arms." Gracie whistled. "You were a woman on a mission. You saved that child from certain death."

"Do that again."

"Do what again?" Gracie asked.

"Whistle. I remember really loud whistle." Sheila covered her ears. "It was so loud, it hurt."

"That was Brady. He was the second hero of the day. He stopped the bull from running after you by whistling and carrying on like a...well...lunatic. All those upper-body workouts paid off. That man hoisted himself over that fence like it was nothing."

Sheila closed her eyes, rewatching the scene unfold before her.

"I need to stand up." Sheila allowed Gracie to support her weight. "I'm okay. I just need to splash some water on my face."

Sheila managed to walk to the bathroom by herself. She looked down at the once-white lace top she'd carefully picked out for a fun afternoon. It was covered in dirt and grass stains. Not that she cared. It was just a shirt. Gunner and Brady were safe and nobody had been hurt. That was what mattered.

She allowed herself a few private moments before she opened the bathroom door. She grabbed a bottle of water from the refrigerator and sat down at the table. Twisting off the cap, she noticed a legal pad with various notes scribbled on it. She slid it toward her, realizing they were a list of rodeo events with this year's dates next to them.

"You've got to be kidding me."

She'd gotten him a job, a better job than she had imagined she'd get him, and he was still planning on competing in a few months.

"What's wrong?" Gracie asked.

The front door opened and Brady entered. He smiled at her. "Sleeping beauty has risen."

"What are these?" Sheila waved the pad in the air. "I think I know the answer, but I want to hear from you."

"Those are events I'm hoping to compete in this year."

"You are the most ungrateful, selfish—" She stopped herself from saying any more for fear she'd wake Gunner. She tossed the pad on the table and stormed across the room. "Your son and I were almost killed by a bull today. You were almost killed by a bull today. Your son watched a bull run you down and you think nothing of entering the ring again."

"You knew this was my plan all along," Brady said.

"You're right, I did. But somewhere, somehow, I stupidly thought that if I got you a job here, you'd want to stay. Big mistake. Huge."

"Whoa. You're the reason Kay asked me to work here?"

"Yes. I am." Sheila crossed her arms. "I asked her to hire you as a helper or to train you to provide hippotherapy. She obviously had a different job in mind. When you told me about the job earlier, it was the first I'd heard of it and I was grateful she thought so highly of you. You're a perfect fit. But you don't care. All you care about is getting back in that damn arena. I don't matter to you. Gunner doesn't matter to you. Your dad and Alice don't matter to you." Sheila took a step back. She wanted to slug him. She couldn't remember ever being so angry with someone for being so careless with their life. "You know what, I'm done. I refuse to watch you destroy your life. We're through."

THE FOLLOWING AFTERNOON Sheila knocked on Dr. Mangone's open office door.

"Do you have a few minutes?" she asked.

"A few." He glanced up at the clock on the wall. "What can I do for you?"

Sheila closed the door behind her.

"This looks serious." Dr. Mangone closed the folder on his desk. "Have a seat and tell me what's wrong."

Sheila had stayed awake all night trying to find a way around what she was about to do, but she'd come up empty. She'd known what she was getting herself into and now she needed to correct her mistake. "I can no longer see Brady Sawyer as a patient."

"This is unusual." He flipped the page of his notepad.

"It is?" Sheila had pored over the American Medical Association guidelines last night along with the Texas Medical Board's and Grace General's policy guidelines. "It's my understanding that if there is a conflict of interest I'm obligated to refuse to treat him further."

"Why don't you start from the beginning and tell me what's going on." He picked up his pen.

Sheila took a deep breath. "Mr. Sawyer has developed romantic feelings toward me and I feel uncomfortable treating him." She exhaled.

He jotted notes on his pad. "Many patients develop crushes on their physicians. Has he made any advances toward you or is this just a feeling that you have? And before you answer, understand that I'm not diminishing anything you're saying. I do need to know the details."

"Mr. Sawyer has kissed me on more than one occasion."

"I see." Dr. Mangone peered over his glasses. "Did he force himself on you?"

She sucked in her bottom lip, knowing this conversation could be the end of her career. "No. It was a mutual attraction that has since ended."

Dr. Mangone removed his glasses, set them on the desk and rubbed his eyes. "Sheila, how could you jeopardize your job like this?"

"I don't know." She'd asked herself that same question a thousand times. "I don't have an answer other than I followed my heart. I was attracted to Brady Sawyer. I know I shouldn't have been. And I tried to stay away from him. But I failed. I've never failed at anything. I made a mistake and I own up to it."

"Are you sure it's really over?" Dr. Mangone asked.

Sheila nodded. "Most definitely." The conflict of interest where her job was concerned was bad enough. She wasn't prepared to deal with his unyielding desire to compete again and his unwillingness to consider the feelings of those around him. "I cannot be involved with somebody who's so careless with his life." Sheila ran her palms down the front of her pants. "He doesn't understand what you and I saw the night he was admitted. He slept through it. We have that vivid image imprinted in our brains—at least I do. I can't stand by and watch somebody I care about destroy himself."

"This sounds like more than just a fleeting romance. This is none of my business and you don't have to answer, but are you in love with Brady Sawyer?"

"No." She raised her chin. "No, I am not." Not anymore, she thought to herself.

"I'll transfer Mr. Sawyer's case over to Dr. Washburn." He scribbled furiously on a form he'd removed from the filing cabinet. "Unfortunately, I won't be able to send you to Dance of Hope anymore."

"I can't see my patients?" She'd known that even if he didn't fire her, she might lose Dance of Hope. She'd prayed there would be some way around it.

"As of today they're not your patients anymore. I can't justify sending a doctor out there just to see one patient. You're officially off Dance of Hope, and I'll need to ask you to keep your distance from the facility for a while. At least as long as Brady Sawyer is residing there. We'll consider reinstatement once he's gone. I'm sorry, Sheila. You knew the repercussions. I won't go to the AMA with this because, dammit, you're a good doctor. You're one of the best surgeons we have here and I know how much you want to get into our fellowship program. I'm going to leave this between Mr. Sawyer, you and me, providing you can reassure me that nobody else knows about this relationship. If this is public knowledge, then it's out of my hands."

"Nobody else knows." *At least no one at the hospi-*

tal. Sheila's heart broke. Hippotherapy had inspired her to become an orthopedic surgeon and now it was gone. Dance of Hope was the only center around. She'd made the biggest mistake of her life and she couldn't take it back. She didn't know which hurt more, walking away from Brady or walking away from Dance of Hope. "I appreciate your keeping this off the record."

"You're human. You're not the first physician it has happened to and you won't be the last. Our patients entrust us with their lives. A relationship beyond that violates that trust. This better not happen again."

"It won't." Sheila would never give her heart so carelessly to a man again.

BRADY WAS STILL annoyed nobody would give him Sheila's cell phone number. He hated that he'd resorted to calling her at work, but she'd left him no choice. He'd had her paged once that morning, she'd taken his call only to chastise him. She'd told him unless it was medically related she couldn't speak with him.

When he'd tried to reach her that afternoon, he was beyond ticked that another doctor had answered her page and informed him that Sheila was no longer his physician. He knew he shouldn't have called her at work, but it wasn't as if he could hop in the car and drive over to her house for a visit. If he had, she'd probably report him for stalking. Regardless, she could have handled the situation much better. He shouldn't have to, but he felt the need to discuss the rodeo schedule she saw yesterday. If she could dismiss him so easily without even talking about it, then maybe he was better off without her. He didn't need anyone's approval. He'd prove them all wrong.

Abby had called in sick that day and Brady had gone ahead with physical therapy on his own. With the exception of working on his reflex speed so that he could drive again, he really didn't need any more therapy. Walking continued to improve his balance and increase his strength. He'd already begun leaving his cane aside when he was at the cottage or in the cafeteria and lounge areas of Dance of Hope.

It was still the first week in August and he refused to spend it indoors. He walked down to the rodeo school and cheered on the incoming session of riders.

"Brady." Shane Langtry, one of the rodeo school owners waved him over from the other side of the round pen.

He made his way past the new students to where Shane was standing.

"Hey, man." Shane shook his hand. "I haven't had a chance to personally apologize for yesterday's incident or to thank you for what you did. I realize my bull charged your kid, and that never should have happened, but you handled yourself like a pro. You were a hell of a lot calmer than I would have been in the same situation. I have a few hours free this evening if you want to squeeze some training in."

"I'd like that." Brady picked up a bull rope from the ground. "I want to run something past you. I have no doubt I'll compete again, but I only have a couple good years left, if that. I'd like to get into teaching and

I wondered if you'd consider bringing me on at some point in the future."

"I've seen you compete on the circuit and I've already seen you schooling some of my students." Shane climbed up the fence and sat on the top rail. "Our August session is our busiest month and we can always use an extra hand or two. How about we try you out and see what happens? You can go through boot camp with the kids, learn the ropes of the school, and it will help you get back in shape to compete. It's a win-win. We'll reevaluate the situation come September."

When Brady had made the suggestion, he'd been thinking a year from now. He couldn't believe the same family had offered him two jobs. "Thanks, man." Brady shook his hand. "I didn't expect you to need me right away, but it's all good. You know your mom hired me to work a couple days a week once my therapy is completed."

"She told me. We'll work something out. I'll need you more in the summer and after school once the season's over with. You could work with my mom when the school isn't in session. And it would still give you plenty of time to compete. I'm assuming you have horses. I don't know what your situation is at home, but if you work for me, I provide stalls for my employees' horses. You're still responsible for everything else they need, but you do get prime Bridle Dance space. I provide a maximum of two stalls per employee. Anything more than that you have to pay for. And if you need a place to live, we have bunkhouses, and we can take your room and board out of your paycheck."

That was an option Brady hadn't known about. Regardless of whether or not he could drive, commuting back and forth to the ranch daily would be a two-hour round-trip. He'd bought his house in January, moved in in February, and was laid up in the hospital by the middle of April. He'd spent a total of two and a half months in the place. He had no real emotional attachment to it.

As for Gunner, he had a room in his mom's apartment and his grandfather's house. When it was Brady's turn to have him he could always stay with him at his dad's.

"Do you mind if I take a day to figure out the logistics?" Brady asked.

"Sure, but how would you feel about jumping in today and teaching these kids a thing or two? I could really use the help."

Brady extended his hand. "It would be my pleasure."

A WEEK LATER and Sheila still couldn't get Brady out of her head. Dr. Washburn had successfully taken over her rounds at Dance of Hope, but according to Gracie, the residents hadn't warmed up to him yet. He'd been there only twice. Sheila was certain once they got used to him, the patients there would develop a similar rapport to what they'd shared with her.

She missed her patients. She missed Brady. She wanted to blame someone, but she couldn't. She was miserable. The fellowship program at Grace General that she'd worked so hard for no longer held the same appeal—she'd specifically chosen the hospital because of its proximity to Dance of Hope. She'd already begun looking for another fellowship near a hippotherapy center. A hospital in northern California looked promising. It was actively involved with a facility similar to Dance of Hope. She'd wait until Brady completed his rehabilitation to see if Dr. Mangone would reinstate her. If not, she'd pursue the other program further. California wasn't ideal, but she needed to prioritize and her career came first. She considered hippotherapy a big part of her future.

Her phone rang in her lab coat pocket. "Dr. Lindstrom speaking."

"Gracie speaking. Can you come out and play or are you still grounded?"

Sheila laughed. Dr. Mangone's punishment sure felt like a grounding. "Is Brady Sawyer still a patient there?"

"For now. I wouldn't be surprised if he was gone by tomorrow. We're not doing much for him anymore. Besides, he spends all his time at the rodeo school."

That figured. Even after everything she'd said and all that had happened, he was still planning to compete. "As long as he's there, I can't be. I don't even know if I'll ever be permitted to work there again."

"You're not allowed to be at Dance of Hope as a physician, but that doesn't include the rest of the ranch. Dance of Hope is just a tiny section of it. Kay makes the rules when it comes to the ranch and she says you're welcome here."

Sheila knew she was right, but she feared she'd run into Dr. Washburn and he'd tell Dr. Mangone he'd seen her at the ranch. After her attending had been gracious enough not to report her to the American Medical Association, she felt it was best to do whatever he asked of her.

"We have a few patients leaving this weekend and we're throwing them a little party tonight. It would be nice if you'd say goodbye to them. I know they would certainly appreciate it."

"If I can get clearance from my attending, I will stop by after work. No promises, Gracie."

"I'm just glad you'll make an attempt," Gracie said. "Let me know what you decide."

A FEW HOURS later Sheila drove through the Bridle Dance Ranch's main entrance gates. Dr. Mangone had given her permission to visit Dance of Hope. He'd also informed her that Dr. Washburn was not thrilled about missing OR time because he had to "play in the dirt." Before she left Dr. Mangone's office, he told her she could return to Dance of Hope once Brady was no longer a patient. She had been so overwhelmed with relief, she'd almost hugged Dr. Mangone—and he was definitely not a huggable man.

She parked and stepped out of her car. The lot seemed unusually silent. The corrals in front of the rodeo school were empty. The arena was empty too. It was quiet. Eerily quiet. Until she entered Dance of Hope.

There were streamers, balloons and cake for the departing residents. Some patients were graduating to different types of therapy facilities while others would probably be back for maintenance therapy. Hippotherapy tended to be ongoing for those with lifelong con-

ditions. As soon as she entered the room, she realized
how much she missed Dance of Hope.

She spent the next hour with her extended family at
the center. She was surprised that, as close as he had
become with many of the residents, Brady was conspicuously absent from the festivities. She wanted to
ask his whereabouts but decided she was better off not
knowing. For all she knew, he was asked to stay away.
Her mind realized Brady's absence was for the best,
but her heart kept looking for a chance encounter. She
felt they owed it to one another to talk. A part of her
even felt the need to apologize for trying to dissuade
him from following his dreams and for not telling him
personally that she would no longer be his physician.

She said her goodbyes and headed toward the combined hippotherapy and rodeo school entrance. As she
entered the foyer separating the two buildings, she heard
whoops and shouts coming from the rodeo school. She
opened the door to the arena and saw Brady astride a
bull in a chute with Shane standing on the platform next
to it, leaning over him. She couldn't see what they were
doing but she knew he was about to ride.

Her stomach dropped when a buzzer sounded and
the chute gate swung wide. The bull charged into the
center of the arena with Brady on his back. Sheila swore
her heart stopped beating as she watched. Granted there
wasn't much bucking going on and the bull essentially
spun in circles before the buzzer sounded again and
Brady jumped off. He landed on his feet and two cowboys quickly jumped in to protect him from the bull as
he made his way to the fence without assistance. Each

deliberate step told Sheila he experienced some discomfort. Even though his walk was two parts limp to one part swagger, it was undeniably testosterone-filled as he climbed over the fence to numerous high fives and congratulatory back slaps.

The reality of the situation smacked her hard in the face. It was one thing for Brady to talk about competing again, but to actually see him in action, even if only on a starter bull, proved too much. Any second thoughts she'd had vanished.

"Thank you, Brady Sawyer," she whispered as she closed the door. "You just saved me from making another mistake."

Chapter Thirteen

October rolled around and two months had passed since Brady had last spoken to Sheila. He'd seen her come and go from Dance of Hope, but she kept her distance and, as a courtesy, he did the same. It hadn't made it any easier. He missed the hell out of her and couldn't understand why they weren't together. But if she couldn't respect his job the way he had respected hers, who needed her? At least that's what he thought until he realized he hadn't exactly respected her job. If he had, he wouldn't have pursued her so relentlessly.

His dad and Alice had agreed with him that selling the ranch and moving into one of the Bridle Dance bunkhouses was a good idea. He was always at his dad's house when Gunner came to visit anyway. Gunner staying over there hadn't been much of a change—it had actually been easier since they weren't constantly running back and forth to visit his father. Within weeks of listing the ranch, he'd accepted an offer close to his asking price. After paying off his mortgage, he didn't have much left over.

At first, both of his new jobs had been a little overwhelming when added to his training schedule. But the diversity ensured he'd never get bored, plus he had a state-of-the-art facility to train in *and* recuperate in should the need arise again.

He'd quit using his cane a few days after Sheila had ended things and refused to see him as a patient any longer. It was rough going at first, but once he'd begun relying solely on his body for support, his recovery had accelerated. He didn't realize how much he'd depended on the cane until he got rid of it.

Living on Bridle Dance had permitted him to work out with the rodeo school students every morning in their fitness center. His treadmill activity had increased from a slow walk to a brisk run and while his body still ached, he'd learned to listen to the pain instead of forcing his way through it. Now he was ready for competition.

There was just one problem. None of it meant anything without Sheila to share it with him. Tonight was his first competitive ride since his accident in April. The Guadalupe County Fair & PRCA Rodeo was in Seguin, Texas, an hour and half southeast of Ramblewood. Even though his family was in attendance, along with Shane and half the rodeo school, Brady kept scanning the stands for Sheila, knowing full well she wouldn't be there. And why should she? Regardless of her saying she wanted him to make a full recovery, the day he knew she'd feared had finally arrived.

Brady's bull was Capone's Revenge. He had a 70 percent buck-off rate. Not too bad a draw for his first time back in the arena. He was also the first ride of the night and that suited him just fine. The opening ceremony had been agony. He was a bundle of nerves and the longer he waited to ride, the more Sheila's fears crept into his head. He needed to shake free of her before he climbed on the bull.

It was time. Months of excruciating hard work had come down to this moment. The anticipation almost unbearable. This was his chance to prove to his fans, sponsors and family that he still had it in him to compete.

In a few minutes it would all be over and he could finally breathe a sigh of relief. "This one's for you, Mom."

SHEILA HADN'T EXPECTED the arena to be so bright. When she heard it was a nighttime rodeo, she'd imagined she and Gracie could sneak in and find seats in the darkness of the opening ceremony. Quite the opposite. The lights in the covered open air arena were on full bore, reflecting off the interior of the white roof. They'd heard Brady's introduction from the parking lot as they walked in. She feared someone from the ranch— or worse, Brady—would spot them. She wished they'd stayed in the parking lot and watched from there. She probably wouldn't have been able to see his ride, but at least she'd be close by if anything happened.

"I'm getting a hot dog." Gracie dug into her pocket for some cash. "Do you want anything?"

"How can you eat at a time like this?" Sheila couldn't even stomach the thought of food, let alone snacking like they were at a baseball game.

"Easy. You surprised me with this impromptu road trip and refused to stop for something to eat on the way, even after I told you I hadn't eaten lunch or dinner. Pardon me if I'm a little hungry."

Sheila shook her head. "Duck down in your seat. I don't want anyone to see us."

"Then what was the point of coming here?" Gracie asked. "There's Alice and Gunner." She raised her hand to wave to them before Sheila swatted it down.

"Stop it." She'd overheard Brady's conversation about tonight's event while she was on rounds at Dance of Hope and immediately roped Gracie into joining her. She'd wanted her friend's support in case Brady's ride ended badly, but now she wondered if it would have been better to come alone. Regardless of which way it went, she had to be there. Had to see him ride for herself, not wait by the telephone for someone to call with the results.

Sheila spotted Brady ascending the stairs to the bull chute platform. "There he is."

The announcer said Brady's name as he climbed over the rails and straddled the bull. Sheila watched him bob up and down a few times as if trying to find a good seat position. Shane stood on the chute platform, his hand in front of Brady's chest while another man held a rope in front of him. Sheila wished she had taken the time to learn more about the sport. But even she knew any bull he rode tonight would have more fire than the rodeo school's starter bull. She was glad he'd at least chosen to wear a helmet. Maybe he had learned something.

After what seemed like an eternity, she saw Brady nod his head. A man stood in the arena holding a rope attached to the chute gate. The hair rose on the back of her neck. She stood to get a better view. The gate swung wide and the massive black bull tore out of the chute. A bell clanged as the animal bucked left then right, almost vertically in no set pattern. The physician in her cringed as she watched Brady's arm wave in the air as he fought to hang on. But the competitor in her broke free and stood on her seat, screaming her head off while cheering him on.

Surely eight seconds had to have passed already. The crowd was on its feet, cheering Brady along with her. Hot tears ran down her face as Gracie squeezed her hand and shouted beside her.

Man against beast and Brady was in control. With the bull's final twist and a kick, Brady flew off and landed low on his hands and feet, then ran for the fence as men in red and purple shirts corralled the animal into another chute.

Thunderous applause rose from the stands. Sheila released the breath she hadn't even known she was holding, along with Gracie's poor hand—7.88 seconds. It felt more like a minute. She'd worked herself into a frenzy for months over 7.88 seconds.

She laughed loudly. Truth be told, she had kind of enjoyed watching him ride. Relief, exhilaration and love for Brady coursed through her veins. She was proud of him. She wanted to hang around and watch the rest of the competition, but she didn't want to risk Brady or anyone else seeing them. Regaining her composure, she resolved it was for the best that no one knew they were there. She and Brady had ended before they'd even really started. She had no right to ask or even want more.

As far as she could tell, they'd gone undetected. She wished she had thought enough ahead to buy baseball hats or some other disguise for her and Gracie.

She nudged her friend's arm. "Come on, let's get out of here."

"We're leaving already? We just got here."

"I saw what I came for."

A 74.5-POINT RIDE was better than Brady had expected for his first time back. It probably wouldn't win him much of anything, but he was okay with that.

Shane slapped him on the back. "You did great out there. How do you feel?"

"Friggin' amazing." Brady was giving his friend a hug when he heard Gunner yell, "Fireworks Lady!" He quickly scanned the crowd, catching sight of two women descending the bleacher stairs over Shane's shoulder. "Is that Sheila and Gracie?" He pointed at them.

"Holy crap." Shane tilted back his hat. "I think it is. Well, what do you know? She couldn't stay away from your first competition. I'd say that means something. What are you waiting for? Catch up to her and celebrate. One of us will drive Gracie back to the ranch."

Shane didn't have to tell Brady twice. If only his body would cooperate—his thighs still quaked from the powerful ride he'd just completed and his fingers fumbled as he unfastened his helmet. Finally, he weaved his way through the competitors waiting to ride behind the bull chutes. But by the time he reached the stands,

Sheila and Gracie were out of sight. Alice called out and waved to him, pointing to the exit.

The Guadalupe County Fair parking lot rivaled the size of the Luna County Fairgrounds where he'd searched for Sheila once before. He ran his hands down his face, not knowing where to begin, when he spotted her car backing out of a parking space.

"Sheila! Gracie!" he called. They didn't hear him and were gone within seconds. "No worries. I have a better idea."

"I CAN'T BELIEVE you're going to ride all the way to her house," Thomas said.

Brady had thought of nothing else since he'd missed catching Sheila last night and had spent the better part of the day working out the logistics of his plan.

"If I was smart, I'd just give you her number, but Gracie would have my head. I still don't understand why you don't borrow a truck and drive over there."

"Because I need to do this on my own." Brady mounted Thomas's mule, Blue.

"Then you should walk," Thomas said. "What's the difference between borrowing Blue and borrowing a vehicle?"

"Because you'll catch hell from your wife for loaning me yours and I don't feel like involving anyone else in this. Besides, Sheila will appreciate the symbolism." At least he hoped she would. If she drove the hour and half to Seguin to see him compete, he could manage twelve miles on the back of a mule. "Trust me. I'm sure Sheila will tell Gracie all about it tomorrow and it'll make sense then. Just make sure Gracie doesn't call the house tonight. Sheila and I have some catching up to do."

"And you're sure you know how to get there?"

Brady nodded. "Wish me luck."

"Break a leg. Well—on second thought, don't. Just be careful. You should be there by sunset. Call me when you're ready to come back and I'll trailer Blue home. Gracie can't yell at me for that."

"Will do." Brady made a clicking sound with his mouth and nudged the mule forward with his knees. He waved his hat in the air shouting "yee haw" as he rode down the main ranch road.

By the time he turned onto Sheila's street, he and Blue had become the best of friends. He'd never considered owning a mule before, but he rather enjoyed the equine hybrid.

He spotted Sheila through her kitchen window standing at the sink. He leaned forward and patted Blue's neck. "There she is. The woman who drove me so crazy, I had to ride you all the way here."

He parked his mule outside her window and waved. The sun was just about to dip below the horizon. If it had been any darker, she might not have seen him. After a flurry of activity in the kitchen, Sheila swung open the side door of the house.

Brady dismounted and attempted to casually lean against Blue as if he were leaning on the hood of a vintage Mustang. It would have worked if Blue hadn't moved, almost causing him to hit the ground.

"Is that Thomas's mule?" Sheila asked, ignoring his stumble.

"Sure is. He loaned Blue to me so I could come see you." Brady lengthened the mule's reins. "I don't have your phone number, your friends won't give it to me and I'm not supposed to call you at the hospital. Blue here was my last resort."

"Don't you have a truck? Last I heard you were cleared to drive."

"I threw a rod and it's been in the shop for a week. That's the beauty of working where you live. You don't need a vehicle to get to work."

"Brady Sawyer, you are certifiably crazy." She thrust her hands on her hips. "What are you even doing here?"

"Aw, come on, Sheila. Won't you admit that just a small part of you is happy to see me?"

"Okay." Sheila stepped off her side porch. "A part of me is happy to see you. The other part still wants to strangle you."

"Must be a pretty small part considering you saw me compete last night." Brady removed his hat. "And no, Thomas didn't tell me. Gunner gave you away. I'm touched by the gesture, but I don't know why you left without bothering to say hello."

"It was just something I had to do." Sheila wrung her hands, not even attempting to deny it. "Can we leave it at that?"

Brady studied her in the setting sun. There was more to the story and he hadn't ridden all the way over just to be dismissed. Brady draped an arm around Blue's neck and whispered into his ear. "I think she's still into me.

What do you think?" The mule snorted. "Thanks a lot, bud." Brady patted the mule's withers. "I could have ridden one of my own horses over here, but I chose Blue for a reason. Mules have a long symbolic history. Some say that they represent the most stubborn and inflexible of creatures. I can relate to that. Others say if you dream about them, you're working through a problem in a relationship."

"We don't have a relationship, Brady." Sheila folded her arms.

"I don't agree. I believe we have a very complicated relationship. But maybe this will change your mind." Brady looked Blue in the eyes. "Let me show you how it's done." He knelt on one knee before her, his heart pounding wildly in his chest. "I know that you still want to strangle me, but I love you, Sheila Lindstrom. You drive me crazy and sober me up all in the same breath. I've tried living without you and the sun doesn't shine as bright. I don't want to ruin your career, but if you're willing to accept me as I am, bull riding and all, I'm willing to wait as long as it takes for you to be my wife. Will you marry me?"

Sheila covered her face with her hands. Brady didn't know whether she was happy or upset with him. She held out her hands to him, urging him to rise. "I never should have asked you to give up your hopes and dreams for me. I love you too much to ever do that to you again. I was the one who was stubborn as a mule. I allowed my fears to get in the way."

Brady lifted her chin with his finger, realizing for the first time how much his hands were shaking. "I want a life with you and my son. If I've learned anything over the past few months, it's that life is precious. We've wasted so much time apart, I don't want to spend another day without you. So what do you say…will you marry me?"

"Brady I would be honored to share the rest of my life with you."

She lifted her mouth to his, and their lips brushed. He'd dreamed of kissing her again since the night they'd spent in each other's arms. No amount of physical recovery compared to the way she made him feel. It had been a long year, but it was finally coming together.

THE FOLLOWING MORNING Sheila knocked on Dr. Mangone's office door.

"Do you have a minute?"

Dr. Mangone hung his head and sighed. "What is it, Dr. Lindstrom?"

She closed the door behind her and approached his desk.

"What is the policy for marrying former patients?" She sucked her lips inward.

Dr. Mangone tossed his pen and glasses onto the desk. "Two months ago you wanted nothing to do with Brady Sawyer—we are talking about Brady Sawyer, right?"

"Of course we are." Sheila frowned. It's wasn't like she'd made a habit out of dating her patients.

"Sheila, you were always my rock. The one I could count on to play by the rules and never give me any trouble. Now you give me heartburn." He poked at his chest.

"Definitely not my intention." Sheila tucked her hair behind her ears and sat on the edge of the chair. "We can wait to get married however long the hospital feels is appropriate. But we would really like to get married on Thanksgiving Eve if it's approved." Sheila clasped her hands in front of her face. "Please approve it."

Dr. Mangone pinched the bridge of his nose. "You know that's not my decision. I will bring it to the chief and the hospital board since a wedding would make your relationship public. You know that very thing I asked you not to do? You went and did it. Hopefully if I explain the entire situation they will overlook your indiscretion, but I can't promise anything." He opened his desk drawer and rummaged through it. "Where are my antacids?"

"When do you think you might—"

"Out!" Dr. Mangone ordered. "I will let you know when I know. Now go."

Sheila ran to the door before he changed his mind. "Thank you!"

"Sheila!"

"Sir?" She turned to face him.

"You better invite me to the wedding."

"Of course." She closed the door behind her and jumped up and down. It was happening. She was really marrying Brady Sawyer.

A WEEK LATER Brady knocked on Gunner's open bedroom door. "Hey, champ. Come on out here. Your mom and I need to talk to you about something."

Alice and Brady had decided to break the news to

Gunner at her apartment. Since Sheila had severed the doctor-patient relationship months prior to their engagement, the hospital board was willing to overlook any perceived indiscretion, providing they were all invited to the wedding.

"Am I in trouble?" Gunner asked.

"Of course not, honey," Alice said. "Your dad and I need to talk to you about our expanding family."

"Am I getting a brother or sister?" Gunner's eyes grew large with excitement.

"No, champ, no brother or sister. At least not yet." Brady lifted him onto his lap. "How would you feel about Sheila joining our family?"

"You mean Doc?"

Brady laughed. "Yes, I mean Doc. Would you be all right with Daddy marrying her?"

"I like her. She gives me cookies and takes me to see fireworks."

"Oh, that's the secret to your heart. Cookies and explosives." Alice tickled his belly.

"And what about you?" Brady asked Alice. He wouldn't feel comfortable bringing another woman into Gunner's life without her blessing. "You've been my best friend for as long as I can remember. Are you okay with this wedding?"

Alice rested her head on Brady's shoulder. "Of course I am. I'm flattered that you asked my opinion, though. I think you two make a great couple and I want you to be happy."

"Then I have a wedding to plan." Brady gave them both a family-size hug. "Why don't I start right now with you two? Gunner, how do you feel about being our ring bearer? All you need to do is hold on to the wedding rings. Can you do that?"

Gunner nodded eagerly.

"What about you, Alice?"

"What about me?" She furrowed her brow.

Brady adored the look of confusion across her face. "How would you like to be my best woman?" he asked.

"You mean stand up for you? How would Sheila feel about that?"

"We've already discussed it and she's fine with it." Brady wrapped an arm around her shoulders. "You've always been a part of my family, Alice. I'd like you to be a part of my wedding too. It would mean a lot to me."

"Does that mean I get to plan a bachelor party?" She playfully jabbed him with her elbow.

"On second thought..."

She punched his arm. "Hey, now."

Brady kissed the top of her head. "Will you do it?"

"I'd be honored to be your best woman."

Their little family unit was far from conventional, but it worked. If he was asked, he'd be honored to return the favor and stand up for Alice when she found her Mr. Right.

"That's all I need—my two besties standing up there with me."

Epilogue

A month and a half later, on Thanksgiving Eve, Sheila stood at the entrance of the church in a sleeveless white lace and satin wedding gown. She'd never considered herself traditional, but she'd always dreamed of a country church wedding.

The doors opened wide as the wedding march began to play. Steadying her nerves, she slid her hand into the crook of her father's arm as he led her down the aisle. Brady stood at the altar with Alice and Gunner. She counted each step in her head, willing herself not to cry until after the ceremony. If anyone had told Sheila she would marry a man who had once lain on her operating table, she would have admitted them for head trauma.

It had been three and a half months since Brady had last used his cane. He'd accomplished everything he'd set out to do and then some. She couldn't have been more proud of the man standing before her. Her father gave her a kiss on the cheek and shook Brady's hand. She handed her bouquet to Gracie—her matron of honor—and joined hands with Brady.

The butterflies had settled. She had no reason for nerves any longer.

This is it. This is our moment.

"Dearly beloved," the preacher began. "Sometimes people come into our lives at the most unexpected times, as did Brady when he ended up in Sheila's emergency room. And in his hour of need, she became his angel of mercy, along with the rest of her trauma team at the hospital. Brady and Sheila's love survived against all odds. They had everything stacked against them from the beginning. But they survived to stand here before you and before God to be joined together in holy matrimony."

Brady lightly squeezed her hand, causing a slight shiver of anticipation to travel up her spine.

"Sheila Lindstrom, do you take this man to be your lawfully wedded husband, for better or worse, for richer or poorer, in sickness and in health, and especially in Brady's case, to bandage him up whenever the need may arise for as long as you both shall live?" Hushed laughter spread throughout the congregation.

"I do."

"And do you, Brady Sawyer, take this woman to be your lawfully wedded wife, for better or worse, for richer or poorer, in sickness and in health and, for the love of all things holy, to stay out of her operating room for as long as you both shall live?"

"I don't know if I can promise that last part," Brady teased.

Sheila squeezed his hand tighter. "You just remember, I put you back together, so I know how to take you apart."

"I do, I do." Brady eagerly agreed. "Can I kiss her now?"

"Keep your britches on," the preacher scolded. "A wedding takes more than eight seconds." After exchanging rings with Gunner's assistance, the preacher continued. "By the power vested in me by the state of Texas, I now pronounce you husband and wife. You may kiss your bride."

Seven and a half months ago, Sheila had fought to save Brady's life. Today he completed hers. He had taught her how to love and experience passion so intensely she couldn't imagine a world without him in it. She'd done everything she'd said she wouldn't—she'd married her bull riding patient and become a stepmother. But she wouldn't change a thing. She smiled up at her husband as his lips joined hers. After all, what was eight seconds here and there in exchange for a lifetime of happiness?

* * * * *

SHEILA'S SUGAR COOKIE RECIPE

Ingredients:
1 pound unsalted butter, softened
4 cups white granulated sugar
4 large eggs
2 tablespoons almond extract
1 teaspoon baking powder
8 cups all-purpose flour

Directions:

Cream butter, sugar, eggs and almond extract together with a mixer. Add baking powder and blend well. Gradually incorporate flour, one cup at a time, into the sugar mixture until the dough forms large pea-sized pieces or until you've added 7 cups of flour. Press dough into a ball with your hands. If the dough sticks to your fingers, continue adding remaining flour, one tablespoon at a time until the ball is soft and is no longer sticky. Wrap tightly in plastic wrap and refrigerate for 1 hour.

Remove cookie dough from the refrigerator and divide into four equal portions. Sprinkle pastry board or a clean countertop with flour and roll dough to a ¼-inch thickness.

Cut cookie shapes with desired cookie cutters and place on a parchment-paper-lined cookie sheet. Once you have formed a complete layer, add another sheet of parchment paper and continue layering your cookies. When you've reached 5 layers, start a new cookie sheet.

Freeze unbaked cookies for a minimum of 30 minutes, but preferably overnight for more intricate designs. Freezing helps the cookies retain their shape.

Preheat oven to 350°F.

Bake cookies in a single layer on parchment-lined cookie sheets, leaving at least a ½ inch of space between cookies. Baking times will vary from 10 to 14 minutes, depending on the size of your cookies. Cookies should be a pale golden color when ready. Do not allow them to brown.

Note:

This recipe can be halved easily. You can change the flavor of your cookies by changing your extract flavor. If using peppermint extract, use slightly less. Yielded number of cookies will vary depending on the size and thickness of your cookies.

SHEILA'S ROYAL ICING RECIPE

Ingredients:
8 tablespoons water
3 tablespoons meringue powder
2 pounds powdered sugar
Gel food coloring in various colors
Lemon juice

Directions:

Add water to bowl. Stir in meringue powder. Add two cups of powdered sugar and mix with a mixer on low. Continue to add more sugar, 1 cup at a time until consistency is very thick and holds its shape. Do not overmix. You want the icing to be stiff, not whipped.

Spoon out desired amount into a separate bowl and gradually incorporate the gel food coloring until the desired color is reached. Add 5 to 10 drops of lemon juice to thin the icing. You'll know the consistency is right when you drag a knife through the icing and it heals itself in less than 7 seconds. Spoon icing into pastry bag and begin decorating.

Notes:

Sheila recommends pastry tip size #2 for piping the outline of the cookie and for flooding the outlined area with icing. The amount of moisture in the air will widely affect the amount of powdered sugar and lemon juice needed for each batch of icing. Always perform the knife test.

MILLS & BOON®

Cherish™

EXPERIENCE THE ULTIMATE RUSH OF FALLING IN LOVE

0816/23

MILLS & BOON®

The Regency Collection – Part 2

GET 2 FREE BOOKS!

Join the London ton for a Regency
season in part 2 of our collection!

Order yours at **www.millsandboon.co.uk/regency2**